By F. Scott Fitzgerald

Novels
THE LOVE OF THE LAST TYCOON   *edited by Matthew J. Bruccoli*
TENDER IS THE NIGHT
THE GREAT GATSBY   *edited by Matthew J. Bruccoli*
THE BEAUTIFUL AND DAMNED
THIS SIDE OF PARADISE

Stories
BITS OF PARADISE   *uncollected stories by F. Scott
and Zelda Fitzgerald*
THE BASIL AND JOSEPHINE STORIES   *edited with an introduction
by Jackson R. Bryer and John Kuehl*
THE PAT HOBBY STORIES   *with an introduction by Arnold Gingrich*
TAPS AT REVEILLE
SIX TALES OF THE JAZZ AGE AND OTHER STORIES   *with an
introduction by Frances Fitzgerald Smith*
FLAPPERS AND PHILOSOPHERS   *with an introduction by
Arthur Mizener*
THE STORIES OF F. SCOTT FITZGERALD   *a selection of 28 stories,
with an introduction by Malcolm Cowley*
BABYLON REVISITED AND OTHER STORIES
THE SHORT STORIES OF F. SCOTT FITZGERALD   *edited and with
a preface by Matthew J. Bruccoli*

Stories and Essays
AFTERNOON OF AN AUTHOR   *with an introduction and notes by
Arthur Mizener*
THE FITZGERALD READER   *with an introduction by
Arthur Mizener*

Letters
F. SCOTT FITZGERALD: A LIFE IN LETTERS   *edited by Matthew J.
Bruccoli with an introduction by Andrew Turnbull*
LETTERS TO HIS DAUGHTER   *with an introduction by Frances
Fitzgerald Smith*
DEAR SCOTT/DEAR MAX   *edited by John Kuehl and Jackson Bryer*

And a Comedy
THE VEGETABLE   *with an introduction by Charles Scribner III*

The Love of
THE LAST TYCOON

A Western

F. SCOTT FITZGERALD

EDITED WITH PREFACE AND NOTES BY
MATTHEW J. BRUCCOLI

SCRIBNER

New York London Toronto Sydney

SCRIBNER
1230 Avenue of the Americas
New York, New York 10020

For information about special discounts for bulk purchases,
please contact Simon & Schuster Special Sales:
1-800-456-6798 or business@simonandschuster.com

First Scribner trade paperback edition 2003

Manufactured in the United States of America

11 13 15 17 19 20 18 16 14 12

Library of Congress Cataloging-in-Publication Data
Fitzgerald, F. Scott (Francis Scott), 1896–1940.
[Last tycoon]
The love of the last tycoon : a western / F. Scott Fitzgerald :
preface and notes by Matthew J. Bruccoli.
p.   cm.—(A Scribner classic)
Originally published as: The last tycoon.
1. Man–woman relationships—California—Los Angeles—Fiction.
2. Motion picture industry—California—Los Angeles—Fiction.
3. Hollywood (Los Angeles, Calif.)—Fiction.   I. Bruccoli, Matthew Joseph, 1931–   . II. Title.
PS3511.I9L3   1994   94-6650   CIP
813'.54—dc20
ISBN-13: 978-0-02-019985-4
ISBN-10:   0-02-019985-6

A NOTE ON THE TITLE

It is problematical to replace the title by which a work has been known for more than fifty years. Nonetheless, the decision has been made because *The Last Tycoon* was not F. Scott Fitzgerald's title: it was assigned by Edmund Wilson when he edited the working drafts in 1941.*

Fitzgerald's only surviving title page reads "STAHR / A Romance." But when Sheilah Graham, Fitzgerald's Hollywood companion, sent his work in progress to Maxwell Perkins, Fitzgerald's loyal editor at Charles Scribner's Sons, she explained:

I don't know whether Scott had discussed titles with you. At first for quite a while, he was going to call it STAHR—which is the name of the book's hero. But about three weeks before he died, he said to me, with a grin—"What do you think of this title?—THE LOVE OF THE LAST TYCOON." My first reaction was "I'm not sure." And he wasn't sure either. But he was going to sit on it, and then submit it to you and see what you thought. In his papers he had written it down as follows:

THE LOVE OF THE LAST TYCOON
A Western
By F. Scott Fitzgerald

The title has grown on me quite a bit. He wanted it to sound like a movie title and completely disguise the tragi-heroic content of the book.

Fitzgerald was writing a western—a novel about the last American pioneers, immigrants, and sons of immigrants who pursued and defined the American dream in the last western frontier. Fitzgerald's

---

*"Tycoon" is the title by which the shogun of Japan was described to foreigners; the earliest *Oxford English Dictionary* citation is 1857. The *OED Supplement* (1986) adds: "An important or dominant person, especially in business or politics; a magnate," noting that "tycoon" was applied to Abraham Lincoln. Its appearances in *Time,* beginning in 1926, gave it currency in America.

manuscript notes include a page headed "Title" on which all of the titles—including "The Last Tycoon"—are crossed out, except for "The Love of the Last Tycoon / A Western," which has a large check mark. Next to this title is a deleted note: "This is the familiar Fitzgerald formula but the boy grows tired." Not too tired.

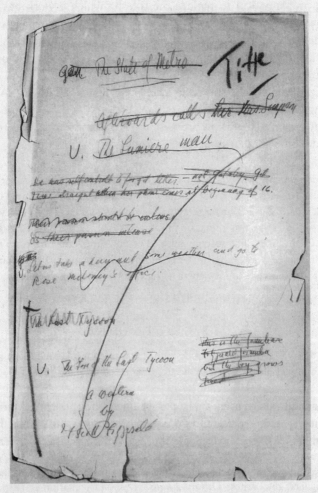

Page from Fitzgerald's working notes. Princeton University Library.

PREFACE*

F. Scott Fitzgerald, a forty-four-year-old unemployed screenwriter, died of a heart attack on 21 December 1940 at 1443 North Hayworth Avenue off Sunset Boulevard in Hollywood. Since the spring of 1939 he had been working on a novel and had drafted seventeen of its thirty projected episodes. Fitzgerald wrote by a process of accretion and revision. The latest working typescripts for these seventeen episodes were preceded by some 100 manuscript and typescript draft episodes. In addition to the working drafts for *The Love of the Last Tycoon*, there are hundreds of pages of notes and plans (see "Selected Fitzgerald Working Notes").

The work in progress edited by Fitzgerald's college friend, the influential critic Edmund Wilson, was published as *The Last Tycoon* in 1941. The text of *The Love of the Last Tycoon* published here supersedes Wilson's edition, which disguises the gestational nature of Fitzgerald's drafts and conveys the impression of a more nearly finished work.

Even in its preliminary and incomplete condition, *The Love of the Last Tycoon* is regarded as the best novel written about the movies. It is not generally recognized that Fitzgerald was also writing one of the few American novels with a convincing and compelling businessman hero. The art of fiction is the art of character. Monroe Stahr is an archetypal American hero, the embodiment of the American Dream: a Jay Gatsby with genius. It is well known that Stahr was based on Irving Thalberg (1899–1936), the "boy wonder" of the movie industry who became head of production at Metro-Goldwyn-Mayer in 1924. But *The Love of the Last Tycoon*

---

*This preface necessarily draws upon my Introduction and editorial apparatus for the novel in the *Cambridge Edition of the Works of F. Scott Fitzgerald* (New York & London: Cambridge University Press, 1993), which necessarily draws upon my book *"The Last of the Novelists": F. Scott Fitzgerald and The Last Tycoon* (Carbondale & Edwardsville: Southern Illinois University Press, 1977).

is not a biographical novel; Monroe Stahr is a fictional character who exemplifies Fitzgerald's essential theme of aspiration.

Fitzgerald did not know Thalberg well, having worked for him—but not with him—briefly and unsatisfactorily. However, the impression that Thalberg made on him at their first encounter in 1927 is preserved in one of Fitzgerald's working notes:

We sat in the old commissary at Metro and he said, "Scottie, supposing there's got to be a road through a mountain—a railroad and two or three surveyors and people come to you and you believe some of them and some of them you don't believe, but all in all, there seem to be half a dozen possible roads through those mountains, each one of which, so far as you can determine, is as good as the other. Now suppose you happen to be the top man, there's a point where you don't exercise the faculty of judgment in the ordinary way, but simply the faculty of arbitrary decision. You say, 'Well, I think we will put the road there' and you trace it with your finger and you know in your secret heart and no one else knows, that you have no reason for putting the road there rather than in several other different courses, but you're the only person that knows that you don't know why you're doing it and you've got to stick to that and you've got to pretend that you know and that you did it for specific reasons, even though you're utterly assailed by doubts at times as to the wisdom of your decision because all these other possible decisions keep echoing in your ear. But when you're planning a new enterprise on a grand scale, the people under you mustn't ever know or guess that you're in any doubt because they've all got to have something to look up to and they mustn't ever dream that you're in doubt about any decision. Those things keep occurring."

At that point, some other people came into the commissary and sat down and the first thing I knew there was a group of four and the intimacy of the conversation was broken, but I was very much impressed by the shrewdness of what he said—something more than shrewdness—by the largeness of what he thought and how he reached it at the age of 26, which he was then.

This encounter was written into the first chapter of the novel as Stahr's lecture to the pilot on responsibility.

When Fitzgerald began writing his Hollywood novel in 1939 he had not published a novel since *Tender Is the Night* in 1934. He was on the MGM payroll from July 1937 to December 1938 but received only one screen credit—for his collaboration on the *Three Comrades* screenplay. After MGM declined to renew his contract he supported his family by occasional brief free-lance screenwriting jobs and short-short stories for *Esquire* magazine. The short-shorts included seventeen stories about Pat Hobby, a broken-down Hollywood hack. These stories are not autobiographical; they are mainly satirical and have no direct connection with the novel Fitzgerald was writing at the same time. He needed financial backing to work on the novel and attempted to obtain an advance from *Collier's* magazine for the pre-book serial rights—that is, to sell the novel before it was written. Accordingly, he sent this prospectus to *Collier's* editor Kenneth Littauer on 29 September 1939:

This will be difficult for two reasons. First that there is one fact about my novel, which, if it were known, would be immediately and unscrupulously plagiarized by the George Kaufmans,* etc., of this world. Second, that I live always in deadly fear that I will take the edge off an idea for myself by summarizing or talking about it in advance. But, with these limitations, here goes:

The novel will be fifty thousand words long. As I will have to write sixty thousand words to make room for cutting I have figured it as a four months job—three months for the writing—one month for revision. The thinking, according to my conscience and the evidence of sixty pages of outline and notes, *has already been done*. I would infinitely rather do it, now that I am well again, then take hack jobs out here.

* * *

The Story occurs during four or five months in the year 1935. It is told by Cecelia, the daughter of a producer named Bradogue in Hollywood. Cecelia is a pretty, modern girl neither good nor bad, tremendously human. Her father is also an important character. A shrewd man, a gentile, and a scoundrel of the lowest variety. A self-made man, he has brought Cecelia up to be a princess, sent her East to college, made of her rather a snob, though, in the course of the story, her character evolves *away from this*. That is, she was twenty when the events that she tells occurred, but she is

*Fitzgerald was convinced that his play *The Vegetable* had provided playwright George S. Kaufman with the idea for *Of Thee I Sing* (1931). *Editor*.

twenty-five when she tells about the events, and of course many of them appear to her in a different light.

Cecelia is the narrator because I think I know exactly how such a person would react to my story. She is *of* the movies but not *in* them. She probably was born the day "The Birth of the Nation" was previewed and Rudolph Valentino came to her fifth birthday party. So she is, all at once, intelligent, cynical but understanding and kindly toward the people, great or small, who are of Hollywood.

She focuses our attention upon two principal characters—Milton [Monroe] Stahr (who is Irving Thalberg—and *this is my great secret*) and Thalia [Kathleen Moore], the girl he loves. Thalberg has always fascinated me. His peculiar charm, his extraordinary good looks, his bountiful success, the tragic end of his great adventure. The events I have built around him are fiction, but all of them are things which might very well have happened, and I am pretty sure that I saw deep enough into the character of the man so that his reactions are authentically what they would have been in life. So much so that he may be recognized—but it will also be recognized that *no single fact is actually true*. For example, in my story he is unmarried or a widower, leaving out completely any complication with Norma.*

In the beginning of the book I want to pour out my whole impression of this man Stahr as he is seen during an airplane trip from New York to the coast—of course, through Cecelia's eyes. She has been hopelessly in love with him for a long time. She is never going to win anything more from him than an affectionate regard, even that tainted by his dislike of her father (parallel the deadly dislike of each other between Thalberg and Louis B. Mayer). Stahr is over-worked and deathly tired, ruling with a radiance that is almost moribund in its phosphorescence. He has been warned that his health is undermined, but being afraid of nothing the warning is unheeded. He has had everything in life except the privilege of giving himself unselfishly to another human being. This he finds on the night of a semi-serious earthquake (like in 1935) a few days after the opening of the story.

It has been a very full day even for Stahr—the bursted water mains, which cover the whole ground space of the lot to the depth of several feet, seems to release something in him. Called over to the outer lot to supervise the salvation of the electrical plant (for like Thalberg, he has a finger in every pie of the vast bakery) he finds two women stranded on the roof of a property farmhouse and goes to their rescue.

*Actress Norma Shearer, Irving Thalberg's widow. *Editor*.

Thalia Taylor is a twenty-six year old widow, and my present conception of her should make her the most glamorous and sympathetic of my heroines. Glamorous in a new way because I am in secret agreement with the public in detesting the type of feminine arrogance that has been pushed into prominence in the case of Brenda Frazier,* etc. People simply do not sympathize deeply with those who have had *all* the breaks, and I am going to dower this girl, like Rosalba in Thackeray's "Rose in the Ring" with "a little misfortune." She and the woman with her (to whom she is serving as companion) have come secretly on the lot through the other woman's curiosity. They have been caught there when the catastrophe occurred.

Now we have a love affair between Stahr and Thalia, an immediate, dynamic, unusual, physical love affair—and I will write it so that you can publish it. At the same time I will send you a copy of how it will appear in book form somewhat stronger in tone.

This love affair is the meat of the book—though I am going to treat it, remember, as it comes through to Cecelia. That is to say by making Cecelia at the moment of her telling the story, an intelligent and observant woman, I shall grant myself the privilege, as Conrad did, of letting her imagine the actions of the characters. Thus, I hope to get the verisimilitude of a first person narrative, combined with a Godlike knowledge of all events that happen to my characters.†

Two events beside the love affair bulk large in the intermediary chapters. There is a definite plot on the part of Bradogue [Brady], Cecelia's father, to get Stahr out of the company. He has even actually and factually considered having him murdered. Bradogue is the monopolist at its worst—Stahr, in spite of the inevitable conservatism of the self-made man, is a paternalistic employer. Success came to him young, at twenty-three, and left certain idealisms of his youth unscarred. Moreover, he is a worker. Figuratively he takes off his coat and pitches in, while Bradogue is not interested in the making of pictures save as it will benefit his bank account.

The second incident is how young Cecelia herself, in her desperate love for Stahr, throws herself at his head. In her reaction at his indifference she gives herself to a man whom she does not love. This episode is *not* absolutely necessary to the serial. It could be tempered but it might be best to eliminate it altogether.

---

*New York celebrity debutante. *Editor.*
†This paragraph indicates that from the start Fitzgerald was concerned with point-of-view. See below, pp. 15–16. *Editor.*

Back to the main theme, Stahr cannot bring himself to marry Thalia. It simply doesn't seem part of his life. He doesn't realize that she has become necessary to him. Previously his name has been associated with this or that well-known actress or society personality and Thalia is poor, unfortunate, and tagged with a middle class exterior which doesn't fit in with the grandeur Stahr demands of life. When she realizes this she leaves him temporarily, leaves him not because he has no legal intentions toward her but because of the hurt of it, the remainder of a vanity from which she had considered herself free.

Stahr is now plunged directly into the fight to keep control of the company. His health breaks down very suddenly while he is on a trip to New York to see the stockholders. He almost dies in New York and comes back to find that Bradogue has seized upon his absence to take steps which Stahr considers unthinkable. He plunges back into work again to straighten things out.

Now, realizing how much he needs Thalia, things are patched up between them. For a day or two they are ideally happy. They are going to marry, but he must make one more trip East to clinch the victory which he has conciliated in the affairs of the company.

Now occurs the final episode which should give the novel its quality— and its unusualness. Do you remember about 1933 when a transport plane was wrecked on a mountain-side in the Southwest, and a Senator was killed? The thing that struck me about it was that the country people rifled the bodies of the dead.* That is just what happens to this plane which is bearing Stahr from Hollywood. The angle is that of three children who, on a Sunday picnic, are the first to discover the wreckage. Among those killed in the accident besides Stahr are two other characters we have met. (I have not been able to go into the minor characters in this short summary.) Of the three children, two boys and a girl, who find the bodies, one boy rifled Stahr's possessions; another, the body of a ruined ex-producer; and the girl, those of a moving picture actress. The possessions which the children find, symbolically determine their attitude toward their act of theft. The possessions of the moving picture actress tend the young girl to a selfish possessiveness; those of the unsuccessful producer sway one of the boys

---

*On 6 May 1935 Senator Bronson M. Cutting and four others were killed when a passenger plane crashed at Atlanta, Missouri. Also aboard were members of a Paramount film crew. The local people aided in rescuing the injured; the wreckage was not plundered. See Richard Lowitt, *Bronson M. Cutting* (Albuquerque: University of New Mexico Press, 1992). *Editor.*

toward an irresolute attitude; while the boy who finds Stahr's briefcase is the one who, after a week, saves and redeems all three by going to a local judge and making full confession.

The story swings once more back to Hollywood for its finale. During the story *Thalia has never once been inside a studio.* After Stahr's death as she stands in front of the great plant which he created, she realizes now that she never will. She knows only that he loved her and that he was a great man and that he died for what he believed in.

This is a novel—not even faintly of the propoganda type. Indeed, Thalberg's opinions were entirely different from mine in many respects that I will not go into. I've long chosen him for a hero (this has been in my mind for three years) because he is one of the half-dozen men I have known who were built on the grand scale. That it happens to coincide with a period in which the American Jews are somewhat uncertain in their morale, is for me merely a fortuitous coincidence. The racial angle shall scarcely be touched on at all. Certainly if Ziegfeld* could be made into an epic figure than what about Thalberg who was literally everything that Ziegfeld wasn't?

There's nothing that worries me in the novel, nothing that seems uncertain. Unlike *Tender is the Night* it is not the story of deterioration—it is not depressing and not morbid in spite of the tragic ending. If one book could ever be "like" another I should say it is more "like" *The Great Gatsby* than any other of my books. But I hope it will be entirely different— I hope it will be something new, arouse new emotions perhaps even a new way of looking at certain phenomena. I have set it safely in a period of five years ago to obtain detachment, but now that Europe is tumbling about our ears this also seems to be for the best. It is an escape into a lavish, romantic past that perhaps will not come again into our time. It is certainly a novel I would like to read. Shall I write it?

Fitzgerald's copy of the letter continues:

As I said, I would rather do this for a minimum price than continue this in-and-out business with the moving pictures where the rewards are great, but the satisafction unsatisfactory and the income tax always mopping one up after the battle.

*Florenz Ziegfeld (1869–1932), producer of lavish annual Broadway shows called *The Ziegfeld Follies*. *Editor.*

The minimum I would need to do this with peace of mind would be $15,000., payable $3000. in advance and $3000. on the first of November, the first of December, the first of January and the first of February, on delivery of the last instalment. For this I would guarantee to do no other work, specifically pictures, to make any changes in the manuscript (but not to have them made for me) and to begin to deliver the copy the first of November, that is to give you fifteen thousand words by that date.

Unless these advances are compatible with your economy, Kenneth, the deal would be financially impossible for me under the present line up. Four months of sickness completely stripped me and until your telegram came I had counted on a build up of many months work here before I could *consider* beginning the novel. Once again a telegram would help tremendously, as I am naturally on my toes and [*the rest is missing*].

Littauer replied on 10 October that he could not make an advance without seeing a "substantial sample of the finished product"— 15,000 words. Fitzgerald needed the advance to write the sample. In November he sent *Collier's* a 6,000-word draft of the first chapter, but the editor declined to support Fitzgerald's further work because the opening was "pretty cryptic." Thereafter Fitzgerald combined writing his novel with money-making work.

Fitzgerald was a meticulous planner and painstaking rewriter of his novels. He wrote in pencil and revised his prose through layers of secretarial typescript: he never typed. Working slowly he had written 44,000 words for five chapters and the opening of the sixth chapter—for a planned nine-chapter novel—when he died. It is necessary to emphasize that he regarded these words as work in progress to be revised and rewritten. After Chapter 1, he wrote episodes to be combined into chapters in a later stage. The latest typescript for Chapter 1 is headed: "Rewrite from mood. Has become stilted with rewriting. Don't look—rewrite from mood." Moreover, these episode drafts are in various states of revision. There is no final typescript for the finished parts of the novel. The surviving text is not just an unfinished novel: it is work in progress toward an unfinished novel—a novel in the process of development and refinement.

* * *

The Love of the Last Tycoon is properly read and judged as a work in progress: drafts in which Fitzgerald had not yet fulfilled his intentions but can be seen working toward them—or perhaps discovering his intentions in the act of writing.

Point-of-view—who tells the story; how it is told; from what perspective it is told—is the fundamental technique of fiction writing. It is the means by which the author controls the reader's response; and it is the means by which the author controls the tone of the work. Tone is the writer's attitude toward the material and therefore the attitude to be developed in the reader. The warmth of Fitzgerald's narrative voice is a defining quality of his prose.

Apart from plotting problems, the most serious difficulty in the drafts involves the use of Cecelia as narrator. There are two voices in the drafts of *The Love of the Last Tycoon*, but the voices of Cecelia and the omniscient narrator are not consistently differentiated. Having succeeded brilliantly with the partially involved narrator Nick Carraway in *The Great Gatsby*, Fitzgerald intended to develop the device further in *The Love of the Last Tycoon*. His prospectus for *Collier's* expresses his plan for using Cecelia's narrative "to get the verisimilitude of a first person narrative, combined with a Godlike knowledge of all events that happen to my characters." This intention is not realized in the drafts, and Cecelia relates events she could not have witnessed. One of Fitzgerald's working notes indicates that he had decided to let the point-of-view inconsistencies stand: "Cecelia does not tell the story though I write it as if she does whenever I can get the effect of looking out." There are two places where Fitzgerald found it necessary to remind the reader that the point-of-view had shifted: "This is Cecelia taking up the narrative in person" (see pp. 77 and 99).

Fitzgerald was a lifelong hero-worshipper, but he was not able to create an unflawed hero until he himself was in his forties. Monroe Stahr is the first hero in a Fitzgerald novel with a successful career: Amory Blaine and Anthony Patch have no occupations; Gatsby's business activities are shadowy; and Dick Diver abandons his promising medical career. But Stahr is totally committed to his work and the responsibility that goes with it. He is Fitzgerald's only complete professional. Moreover, Stahr is immune to the emotional bankruptcy that is epidemic in Fitzgerald's work after 1930. A lonely young widower with a pervasive sense of loss, Stahr is nonetheless not broken by loss, and he retains the capacity to love again. Stahr's one terrible mistake comes when he delays the decision to go away with Kathleen by one day—and during that day he loses her. If one is compelled to seek a flaw in Stahr, it is that he has an excess of reason or discipline; but it would be difficult to support this reading.

One of the familiar lines of Fitzgerald criticism is that his women are tougher than his men; that in what almost amounts to a reversal of traditional sexual roles, the men tend to be romantically weak, whereas the women are strong. In *The Love of the Last Tycoon* Fitzgerald created his only strong novel hero. As a consequence, perhaps, the characterization of Kathleen is not compelling. Stahr so commands the reader's attention and imagination that no one else in the novel can compete with him. It is possible that at forty-four Fitzgerald no longer felt as keenly about women as he once had. That Fitzgerald sensed a deficiency in his treatment of Kathleen is revealed by his note: "Where will the warmth come from in this. Why does he think she's warm. Warmer than the voice in Farewell. My girls were all so warm and full of promise. The sea at night. What can I do to make it honest and different?"

A clue to Fitzgerald's difficulties with Kathleen is provided by his working title: *The Love of the Last Tycoon*. The novel has a split focus. It is a love story and a character study of an American archetype. Stahr dominates the novel, and the strongest scenes are those that show him at work. There are many ironies in Fitzgerald's career, but none is more eloquent than that the "laureate of the Jazz Age" became the admiring creator of a worker-boss. Nevertheless, this irony is not surprising in view of Fitzgerald's lifelong respect for achievement and his guilt about his own irresponsibility.

Endings

Because it was necessary for Fitzgerald to interrupt work on the novel for income-generating writing, he prepared a careful outline-plan. The nine-chapter organization in the first column divides the chapters in thirty episodes, with a chronology and projected word counts. The middle column notes the principal action and function of each chapter. The third column provides a five-act structure. Although Fitzgerald had written seventeen episodes when he died, he had only started the third act. The novel was growing as he wrote, and the 51,000-word projection was no longer accurate.

Fitzgerald's outline-plan is supplemented by Sheilah Graham's 6 March 1941 report to Wilson:

This is how it was going to end:

Brady was out to ruin Stahr in the same way that at one time, and perhaps all the time, L. B. Mayer was out to wrest control of Metro from and/or to ruin Irving Thalberg. Stahr was almost kicked out and decided to remove Brady. He resorted to Brady's own gangster methods—he was going to have him murdered.

On a 'plane flying back to Hollywood Stahr decides not to go through with the murder, which has already been planned and which other people are doing for him—if he did, he would be as bad as the Brady crowd. So at the next airplane stop he plans a cancellation of orders. I imagine the murder was to take place within a few hours. Before the next stop, however, the 'plane crashes, and Stahr is killed. Which left the murder to go through.

I think the final scene of all was to have been Stahr's funeral. And Scott was going to use an actual incident that happened at Thalberg's funeral. Harry Carey, a well-known actor in the old silents and popular in the early talkies, had been unable to get a job in pictures for several years before Thalberg died. He did not know Thalberg and was surprised to receive an invitation to act as pallbearer at his funeral. It was considered a great honor and only the most important and most intimate of Thalberg's friends (all of them important) were asked to be pallbearers. Harry Carey—slightly dazed, accepted and big-shots at the funeral were amazed when they saw Carey, presuming he had an inside track of some sort with Thalberg, and as a direct result he was deluged with picture offers and has been working

Episodes		

A 1. The plane   June 28
  2. Nashville
  3. Up Forward. Different
             6000
	Chapter (A) Introduce
	Cecelia, Stahr, White,
	Schwartze.
		Act I June
		(THE PLANE)
		    6000
		
		STAHR

B 4. Johnny Swanson--Marcus leaving
    --Brady   July 28th.
  5. The Earthquake
  6. The Back lot   3000
	Chapter (B) Introduces
	Brady, Kathleen, Robinson
	and secretaries. Atmos-
	phere of night-sustain
		Act II
		(THE CIRCUS
		July--early August
		    21,000

C 7. The Camera man.   July 29
    Stahr's work and health. From
    something she wrote
  8. First Conference
  9. Second conference and afterwards.
  10. Commissary and Idealism about non-
    profit pictures. Rushes Phone call,
    etc.
          5000
	Chapters (C) & (D) are
	equal to guest list and
	Gatsby's party. Throw
	everything into this, with
	selection. They must have
	a plot, though, leading to
	13
		STAHR AND KATHLEEN

D 11. Visit to rushes.
  12. Second Meeting that night.
    Wrong girl--glimpse
          2500		

E 13. Cecelia and Stahr and Ball - Aug. 6th
    Football game. Cecelia and
         Wylie and Maude.
  14. Malibu seduction. Try to get on lot.
     DEAD MIDDLE
  15. Cecelia and father
  16. Phone call & Wedding.   6000
	Chapter (E) Three episodes
	Atmosphere in 15 most
	important. Hint of Waste
	Land of the house too late.	

F 17. The Damn breaks with Brimmer
  18. The Cummerbund - market--
    (The theatre with Benchley)
              August 10th
  19. The four meet, like Hop and Lofty.
    Renewal. Palomar
  20. Wylie White in Office
        August 28th-Sept. 14th.
	Chapter (F) This belongs
	to the women. It introduces
	Smith (for the 1st time?)
		Act III Aug-early
		Sept.
		(The Underworld)
		    11,500
		
		THE STRUGGLE

G 21. Sick in Washington. To quit?
  22. Brady and Stahr--double blackmail.
    Quarrel with Wylie.
  23. Throws over Cecelia who tells her
    father. Stops making pictures.
    A story conference--rushes and
    sets. Lies low after Cut.
  24. Last fling with Kathleen. Old
    stars in heat wave at Encino.
        6500
	Chapter (G) The blows
	fall on Stahr. Sense of
	heat all through, culmina-
	ting in 25.	

H 25. Brady gets to Smith, Fleishacker
    and Cecelia. (S.G.&K)
        Sept. 15-30th.
  26. Stahr hears plan. Camera man O.K.
    Stops it--very sick.
  27. Resolve problem. Thalia at airport.
    Cecelia to college; Thalia at
    airport. S.G.
        7000
	Chapter (H). The suit and
	the price.
		Act IV September
		(The Murderers)
		    7000
		DEFEAT

I 28. The Plane falls. Fortaste of the
    future in Fleishacker
        Sept 30th-Oct.
  29. Outside the studio. S.G.
  30. Johnny Swanson at funeral
      4500
	Chapter (I) Stahr's death.	Act V October
		(The End)
		    4500
		
		EPILOGUE

WRITTEN FOR TWO PEOPLE - FOR SF AT 17 AND FOR EW AT 45 - IT MUST PLEASE THEM BOTH   51,000

Latest outline-plan. The note at the bottom refers to Scottie Fitzgerald and
Edmund Wilson; SG is Sheilah Graham. (F. Scott Fitzgerald Papers, Princeton University Library)

ever since. The invitation was a mistake. It was meant for someone else, whom Scott told me about but whose name I have forgotten.*

Scott was going to have at the funeral all the Hollywood hypocrites assembled in full force. I had told him of the Marx Brothers sobbing their eyes out on the day Thalberg died—always making sure they were within crying distance of the "right" people. Scott was going to have Stahr's spirit say, "Trash!"

The English girl was to remain an outsider in Hollywood—I think one of Scott's notes has that she would never get inside a studio (although that is where Stahr first saw her on that idol floating down with the flood). Cecelia, that narrator, is writing her story in a sanitarium for T.B.'s, and this, of course, would be revealed at the end.

At the point where Scott left off things were to go badly for Stahr in business and love. Many things, although in the plan, would have been changed in the same way that he deviated within the structure of the plot on what he had already written and the plan. In the plan he had the American man the English girl married, a technician or something in the studio. But I think he was going to change that—make him more powerful, put him in the position of damaging Stahr.

As planned, the novel had an ending (the plane crash) followed by an epilogue (Kathleen and the funeral).

However, Graham's account does not necessarily provide Fitzgerald's final plot. It is unlikely that he had decided how the novel would continue. As late as 2 November 1940—less than two months before his death—he wrote to his wife, Zelda, that the novel "is still in the early character-planting stage." This statement applies to Robinson and Zavras, who were obviously planted for plot purposes to be utilized in the unwritten episodes. Zavras's last speech to Stahr in Episode 11 is: "If you want anybody's throat cut anytime day or night . . . my number is in the book."

· · ·

The 1941 publication of Edmund Wilson's edition of this novel in a volume with *The Great Gatsby* and short stories elicited Stephen

---

*One of Fitzgerald's notes reads: "Harry Cary gets Cary Wilson's invite. A new career." Both Harry Carey and writer Carey Wilson were pallbearers at Thalberg's funeral. The widely reported anecdote is disputed in Bob Thomas's *Thalberg* (Garden City, NY: Doubleday, 1969). *Editor.*

Vincent Benét's prescient declaration: "You can take off your hats now, gentlemen, and I think perhaps you had better. This is not a legend, this is a reputation—and, seen in perspective, it may well be one of the most secure reputations of our time." In the half-century since then, F. Scott Fitzgerald's incomplete work has come to be regarded as the most promising—and the most disappointing—fragment in American fiction. The purpose of the present edition of *The Love of the Last Tycoon: A Western* is to foster the proper assessment of the work in progress as a work of art.

Editorial Note

Just as a work in progress requires special reading, so does it require appropriate editing. The rationale for this edition of *The Love of the Last Tycoon* is to provide a trustworthy reading text that preserves the form and organization of Fitzgerald's latest working typescripts while correcting typographical and factual errors that he expected to be corrected before publication of the completed novel. Thus the surviving episodes have not been combined into chapters, but nonfunctional errors* have been emended. Fitzgerald was a social realist. There is abundant evidence that he wanted to get details right. The many errors in his published books resulted from the lack of editorial help Fitzgerald expected and required. It is not an act of literary piety to protect and perpetuate obvious errors that distract careful readers. The proper function of a critical edition is to fulfill the author's clear intentions. The corrections in this edition involve only word substitutions: see Explanatory Note on Greek culture, 61.10–11. *Fitzgerald's prose has not been rewritten.*

Fitzgerald spelled and punctuated by ear. The misspellings have been corrected; in a few cases it was necessary to decide which word he was trying to spell. Fitzgerald's spellings of his characters' names have been retained, except for the Greek cameraman Pete

---

*A nonfunctional error is not deliberate and serves no purpose in the work; a functional error is intentional and purposeful in the interior world of the fiction.

Zavras, who is called Pedro Garcia in the drafts—almost certainly an authorial private joke. Fitzgerald's punctuation, which indicates the prose rhythms he heard as he wrote, has been retained when not potentially confusing. He was a light punctuator who rationed commas and preferred dashes to colons or semicolons. Fitzgerald never mastered the rules for punctuating dialogue, and these flaws have been corrected here. Despite a policy of conservative emendation, this new text of *The Love of the Last Tycoon* makes 843 emendations of words and punctuation in the typescript of the latest working drafts.

MATTHEW J. BRUCCOLI
The University of South Carolina
1993

The Love of
THE LAST
TYCOON

CHAPTER I

Though I haven't ever been on the screen I was brought up in pictures. Rudolph Valentino came to my fifth birthday party—or so I was told. I put this down only to indicate that even before the age of reason I was in a position to watch the wheels go round.

I was going to write my memoirs once, "The Producer's Daughter," but at eighteen you never quite get around to anything like that. It's just as well—it would have been as flat as an old column of Lolly Parsons'. My father was in the picture business as another man might be in cotton or steel, and I took it tranquilly. At the worst I accepted Hollywood with the resignation of a ghost assigned to a haunted house. I knew what you were supposed to think about it but I was obstinately unhorrified.

This is easy to say, but harder to make people understand. When I was at Bennington some of the English teachers who pretended an indifference to Hollywood or its products really *hated* it. Hated it way down deep as a threat to their existence. Even before that, when I was in a convent, a sweet little nun asked me to get her a script of a screen play so she could "teach her class about movie writing" as she had taught them about the essay and the short story. I got the script for her and I suppose she puzzled over it and puzzled over it but it was never mentioned in class and she gave it back to me with an air of offended surprise and not a single comment. That's what I half expect to happen to this story.

You can take Hollywood for granted like I did, or you can dismiss it with the contempt we reserve for what we don't understand. It can be understood too, but only dimly and in flashes. Not half a dozen men have ever been able to keep the whole equation of pictures in their heads. And perhaps the closest a woman can come to the set-up is to try and understand one of those men.

The world from an airplane I knew. Father always had us travel back and forth that way from school and college. After my sister died when I was a junior, I travelled to and fro alone and the journey always made me think of her, made me somewhat solemn and subdued. Sometimes there were picture people I knew on board the plane, and occasionally there was an attractive college boy—but not often during the Depression. I seldom really fell asleep during the trip, what with thoughts of Eleanor and the sense of that sharp rip between coast and coast—at least not till we had left those lonely little airports in Tennessee.

This trip was so rough that the passengers divided early into those who turned in right away and those who didn't want to turn in at all. There were two of these latter right across from me and I was pretty sure from their fragmentary conversation that they were from Hollywood—one of them because he looked like it, a middle-aged Jew who alternately talked with nervous excitement or else crouched as if ready to spring, in a harrowing silence; the other a pale, plain, stocky man of thirty, whom I was sure I had seen before. He had been to the house or something. But it might have been when I was a little girl, and so I wasn't offended that he didn't recognize me.

The stewardess—she was tall, handsome and flashing dark, a type that they seemed to run to—asked me if she could make up my berth.

"—and, dear, do you want an aspirin?" She perched on the side of the seat and rocked precariously to and fro with the June hurricane, "—or a Nembutal?"

"No."

"I've been so busy with everyone else that I've had no time to ask you." She sat down beside me and buckled us both in. "Do you want some gum?"

This reminded me to get rid of the piece that had been boring me for hours. I wrapped it in a piece of magazine and put it into the automatic ash-holder.

"I can always tell people are nice—" the stewardess said approvingly "—if they wrap their gum in paper before they put it in there."

We sat for a while in the half-light of the swaying car. It was vaguely like a swanky restaurant at that twilight time between meals. We were all lingering—and not quite on purpose. Even the stewardess, I think, had to keep reminding herself why she was there.

She and I talked about a young actress I knew, whom she had flown west with two years before. It was in the very lowest time of the Depression and the young actress kept staring out the window in such an intent way that the stewardess was afraid she was contemplating a leap. It appeared though that she was not afraid of poverty, but only of revolution.

"I know what Mother and *I* are going to do," she confided to the stewardess. "We're coming out to the Yellowstone and we're just going to live simply till it all blows over. Then we'll come back. They don't kill artists—you know?"

The proposition pleased me. It conjured up a pretty picture of the actress and her mother being fed by kind Tory bears who brought them honey, and by gentle fawns who fetched extra milk from the does and then lingered near to make pillows for their heads at night. In turn I told the stewardess about the lawyer and the director who told their plans to Father one night in those brave days. If the bonus army conquered Washington the lawyer had a boat hidden in the Sacramento River, and he was going to row upstream for a few months and then come back "because they always needed lawyers after a revolution to straighten out the legal side."

The director had tended more toward defeatism. He had an old suit, shirt and shoes in waiting—he never did say whether they were his own or whether he got them from the prop department—and he was going to Disappear into the Crowd. I remember Father saying: "But they'll look at your hands! They'll know you haven't done manual work for years. And they'll ask for your union card." And I remember how the director's face fell, and how gloomy he was while he ate his dessert, and how funny and puny they sounded to me.

"Is your father an actor, Miss Brady?" asked the stewardess. "I've certainly heard the name."

At the name Brady both the men across the aisle looked up. Sidewise—that Hollywood look, that always seems thrown over one shoulder. Then the young, pale, stocky man unbuttoned his safety strap and stood in the aisle beside us.

"Are you Cecelia *Brad*y?" he demanded accusingly, as if I'd been holding out on him. "I *thought* I recognized you. I'm Wylie White."

He could have omitted this—for at the same moment a new voice said, "Watch your step, Wylie!" and another man brushed by him in the aisle and went forward in the direction of the cockpit. Wylie White started, and a little too late called after him defiantly.

"I only take orders from the pilot."

I recognized the kind of pleasantry that goes on between the powers in Hollywood and their satellites.

The stewardess reproved him:

"Not so loud, please—some of the passengers are asleep."

I saw now that the other man across the aisle, the middle-aged Jew, was on his feet also, staring, with shameless economic lechery, after the man who had just gone by. Or rather at the back of the man, who gestured sideways with his hand in a sort of farewell, as he went out of my sight.

I asked the stewardess: "Is he the as*sis*tant pilot?"

She was unbuckling our belt, about to abandon me to Wylie White.

"No. That's Mr. Smith. He has the private compartment, the 'bridal suite'—only he has it alone. The assistant pilot is always in uniform." She stood up. "I want to find out if we're going to be grounded in Nashville."

Wylie White was aghast.

"Why?"

"It's a storm coming up the Mississippi Valley."

"Does that mean we'll have to stay here all *night*?"

"If this keeps up!"

A sudden dip indicated that it would. It tipped Wylie White into the seat opposite me, shunted the stewardess precipitately down in the direction of the cockpit, and plunked the Jewish man into a sitting position. After the studied, unruffled exclamations of distaste that befitted the air-minded, we settled down. There was an introduction.

"Miss Brady—Mr. Schwartze," said Wylie White. "He's a great friend of your father's too."

Mr. Schwartze nodded so vehemently that I could almost hear him saying, "It's true. As God is my judge, it's true!"

He might have said this right out loud at one time in his life—but he was obviously a man to whom something had happened. Meeting him was like encountering a friend who has been in a fist fight or collision, and got flattened. You stare at your friend and say: "What happened to you?" And he answers something unintelligible through broken teeth and swollen lips. He can't even tell you about it.

Mr. Schwartze was physically unmarked; the exaggerated Persian nose and oblique eye-shadow were as congenital as the tip-tilted Irish redness around my father's nostrils.

"Nashville!" cried Wylie White. "That means we go to a hotel. We don't get to the coast till tomorrow night—if then. My God! I was born in Nashville."

"I should think you'd like to see it again."

"Never—I've kept away for fifteen years. I hope I'll *never* see it again."

But he would—for the plane was unmistakably going down, down, down, like Alice in the rabbit hole. Cupping my hand against the window I saw the blur of the city far away on the left. The green sign "Fasten your belts—No smoking" had been on since we first rode into the storm.

"Did you hear what she said?" said Mr. Schwartze from one of his fiery silences across the aisle.

"Hear what?" asked Wylie.

"Hear what he's calling himself," said Schwartze. "Mr. *Smith*!"

"Why not?" asked Wylie.

"Oh nothing," said Schwartze quickly. "I just thought it was funny, Smith." I never heard a laugh with less mirth in it: "Smith!"

I suppose there has been nothing like the airports since the days of the stage-stops—nothing quite as lonely, as somber-silent. The old red-brick depots were built right into the towns they marked —people didn't get off at those isolated stations unless they lived there. But airports lead you way back in history like oases, like the stops on the great trade routes. The sight of air travellers strolling in ones and twos into midnight airports will draw a small crowd any night up to two. The young people look at the planes, the older ones look at the passengers with a watchful incredulity. In the big transcontinental planes we were the coastal rich, who casually alighted from our cloud in mid-America. High adventure might be among us, disguised as a movie star. But mostly it wasn't. And I always wished fervently that we looked more interesting than we did—just as I often have at premieres, when the fans look at you with scornful reproach because you're not a star.

On the ground Wylie and I were suddenly friends, because he held out his arm to steady me when I got out of the plane. From then on, he made a dead set for me—and I didn't mind. From the moment we walked into the airport it had become plain that if we were stranded here we were stranded here together. (It wasn't like the time I lost my boy—the time my boy played the piano with that girl Reina in a little New England farm house near Bennington, and I realized at last I wasn't wanted. Guy Lombardo was on the air playing "Top Hat" and "Cheek to Cheek" and she taught him the melodies. The keys falling like leaves and her hand splayed over his as she showed him a black chord. I was a freshman then.)

When we went into the airport Mr. Schwartze was along with us too but he seemed in a sort of dream. All the time we were trying to get accurate information at the desk he kept staring at the door that led out to the landing field, as if he were afraid the plane would leave without him. Then I excused myself for a few minutes and something happened that I didn't see but when I came back he and White were standing close together, White talking and Schwartze looking twice as much as if a great truck had just backed up over him. He didn't stare at the door to the landing field anymore. I heard the end of Wylie White's remark. . . .

"—I told you to shut up. It serves you right."

"I only said—"

He broke off as I came up and asked if there was any news. It was then half past two in the morning.

"A little," said Wylie White. "They don't think we'll be able to start for three hours anyhow, so some of the softies are going to a hotel. But I'd like to take you out to The Hermitage, Home of Andrew Jackson."

"How could we see it in the dark?" demanded Schwartze.

"Hell, it'll be sunrise in two hours."

"You two go," said Schwartze.

"All right—you take the bus to the hotel. It's still waiting—*he's* in there." Wylie's voice had a taunt in it. "Maybe it'd be a good thing."

"No, I'll go along with you," said Schwartze hastily.

We took a taxi in the sudden country dark outside, and he seemed to cheer up. He patted my kneecap encouragingly.

"I should go along," he said. "I should be chaperone. Once upon a time when I was in the big money, I had a daughter—a beautiful daughter."

He spoke as if she had been sold to creditors as a tangible asset.

"You'll have another," Wylie assured him. "You'll get it all back. Another turn of the wheel and you'll be where Cecelia's papa is, won't he, Cecelia?"

"Where is this Hermitage?" asked Schwartze presently. "Far away at the end of nowhere? Will we miss the plane?"

"Skip it," said Wylie. "We ought to've brought the stewardess along for you. Didn't you admire the stewardess? *I* thought she was pretty cute."

We drove for a long time over a bright level countryside, just a road and a tree and a shack and a tree, and then suddenly along a winding twist of woodland. I could feel even in the darkness that the trees of the woodland were green—that it was all different from the dusty olive-tint of California. Somewhere we passed a Negro driving three cows ahead of him, and they mooed as he scatted them to the side of the road. They were real cows, with warm fresh, silky flanks and the Negro grew gradually real out of the darkness with his big brown eyes staring at us close to the car, as Wylie gave him a quarter. He said "*Thank* you—thank you" and stood there and the cows mooed again into the night as we drove off.

I thought of the first sheep I ever remember seeing—hundreds of them, and how our car drove suddenly into them on the back lot of the old Laemmle studio. They were unhappy about being in pictures but the men in the car with us kept saying:

"Swell?"

"Is that what you wanted, Dick?"

"Isn't that swell?" And the man named Dick kept standing up in the car as if he were Cortez or Balboa, looking over that grey fleecy undulation. If I ever knew what picture they were in I have long forgotten.

We had driven an hour. We crossed a brook over an old rattly iron bridge laid with planks. Now there were roosters crowing and blue-green shadows stirring every time we passed a farm house.

"I told you it'd be morning soon," said Wylie. "I was born near here—the son of impoverished southern paupers. The family mansion is now used as an outhouse. We had four servants—my father, my mother and my two sisters. I refused to join the guild, and so I went to Memphis, to start my career, which has now reached a dead end." He put his arm around me. "Cecelia, will you marry me, so I can share the Brady fortune?"

He was disarming enough so I let my head lie on his shoulder.

"What do you do, Celia? Go to school?"

"I go to Bennington. I'm a junior."

"Oh, I beg your pardon. I should have known but I never had the advantage of college training. But a *jun*ior—why I read in 'Esquire' that juniors have nothing to learn, Cecelia."

"Why do people think that college girls—"

"Don't apologize—knowledge is power."

"You'd know from the way you talk that we were on our way to Hollywood," I said. "It's always years and years behind the time."

He pretended to be shocked.

"You mean girls in the East have no private lives?"

"That's the point. They *have* got private lives. You're bothering me, let go."

"I can't. It might wake Schwartze, and I think this is the first sleep he's had for weeks. Listen, Cecelia, I once had an affair with the wife of a producer. A very short affair. When it was over she said to me in no uncertain terms, she said: 'Don't you ever tell about this or

I'll have you thrown out of Hollywood. My husband's a much more important man than you.' "

I liked him again now, and presently the taxi turned down a long lane fragrant with honeysuckle and narcissus and stopped beside the great grey hulk of the Andrew Jackson house. The driver turned around to tell us something about it but Wylie shushed him, pointing at Schwartze, and we tiptoed out of the car.

"You can't get into the Mansion now," the taxi man told us politely.

Wylie and I went and sat against the wide pillars of the steps.

"What about Mr. Schwartze?" I asked. "Who is he?"

"To hell with Schwartze. He was the head of some combine once—First National? Paramount? United Artists? Now he's down and out. But he'll be back. You can't flunk out of pictures unless you're a dope or a drunk."

"You don't like Hollywood," I suggested.

"Yes I do. Sure I do. Say! This isn't anything to talk about on the steps of Andrew Jackson's house—at dawn."

"I *like* Hollywood," I persisted.

"It's all right. It's a mining town in lotus land. Who said that? I did. It's a good place for toughies but I went there from Savannah, Georgia. I went to a garden party the first day. My host shook hands and left me. It was all there—that swimming pool, green moss at two dollars an inch, beautiful felines having drinks and fun—

"—And nobody spoke to me. Not a soul. I spoke to half a dozen people but they didn't answer. That continued for an hour, two hours—then I got up from where I was sitting and ran out at a dog trot like a crazy man. I didn't feel I had any rightful identity until I got back to the hotel and the clerk handed me a letter addressed to me in my name."

Naturally I hadn't ever had such an experience, but looking back on parties I'd been to, I realized that such things could happen. We don't go for strangers in Hollywood unless they wear a sign saying that their axe has been thoroughly ground elsewhere, and that in any case it's not going to fall on our necks—in other words unless they're a celebrity. And they'd better look out even then.

"You should have risen above it," I said smugly. "It's not a slam at *you* when people are rude—it's a slam at the people they've met before."

"Such a pretty girl—to say such wise things."

There was an eager to-do in the eastern sky, and Wylie could see me plain—thin with good features and lots of style, and the kicking fetus of a mind. I wonder what I looked like in that dawn, five years ago. A little rumpled and pale, I suppose, but at that age, when one has the young illusion that most adventures are good, I needed only a bath and a change to go on for hours.

Wylie stared at me with really flattering appreciation—and then suddenly we were not alone. Mr. Schwartze wandered apologetically into the pretty scene.

"I fell upon a large metal handle," he said, touching the corner of his eye.

Wylie jumped up.

"Just in time, Mr. Schwartze," he said. "The tour is just starting. Home of Old Hickory—America's tenth president. The victor of New Orleans, opponent of the National Bank, and inventor of the Spoils System."

Schwartze looked toward me as toward a jury.

"There's a writer for you," he said. "Knows everything and at the same time he knows nothing."

"What's that?" said Wylie, indignant.

It was my first inkling that he was a writer. And while I like writers—because if you ask a writer anything you usually get an answer—still it belittled him in my eyes. Writers aren't people exactly. Or, if they're any good, they're a whole *lot* of people trying so hard to be one person. It's like actors, who try so pathetically not to look in mirrors. Who lean *back*ward trying—only to see their faces in the reflecting chandeliers.

"Ain't writers like that, Celia?" demanded Schwartze. "I have no words for them. I only know it's true."

Wylie looked at him with slowly gathering indignation. "I've heard that before," he said. "Look, Mannie, I'm a more practical man than you any day! I've sat in an office and listened to some mystic stalk up and down for hours spouting tripe that'd land him on a nut-farm anywhere outside of California—and then at the end tell me how *prac*tical he was, and *I* was a dreamer—and would I kindly go away and made sense out of what he'd said."

Mr. Schwartze's face fell into its more disintegrated alignments. One eye looked upward through the tall elms: He raised his hand and bit without interest at the cuticle on his second finger. There was a bird flying about the chimney of the house and his glance followed it. It perched on the chimney pot like a raven and Mr. Schwartze's eyes remained fixed upon it as he said: "We can't get in. And it's time for you two to go back to the plane."

It was still not quite dawn. The Hermitage looked like a nice big white box, but a little lonely, and vacated still, after a hundred years. We walked back to the car—only after we had gotten in, and Mr. Schwartze had surprisingly shut the taxi door on us, did we realize he didn't intend to come along.

"I'm not going to the Coast—I decided that when I woke up. So I'll stay here, and afterwards the driver could come back for me."

"Going back East?" said Wylie with surprise. "Just because—"

"I have decided," said Schwartze, faintly smiling. "Once I used to be a regular man of decision—you'd be surprised." He felt in his pocket, as the taxi driver warmed up the engine. "Will you give this note to Mr. Smith?"

"Shall I come in two hours?" the driver asked Schwartze.

"Yes . . . sure. I shall be glad to entertain myself looking around."

I kept thinking of him all the way back to the airport—trying to fit him into that early hour and into that landscape. He had come a long way from some ghetto to present himself at that raw shrine. Mannie Schwartze and Andrew Jackson—it was hard to say them in the same sentence. It was doubtful if he knew who Andrew Jackson was as he wandered around, but perhaps he figured that if people had preserved his house Andrew Jackson must have been someone who was large and merciful, able to understand. At both ends of life man needed nourishment—a breast—a shrine. Something to lay himself beside when no one wanted him further, and shoot a bullet into his head.

Of course we did not know this for twenty hours. When we got to the airport we told the purser that Mr. Schwartze was not continuing, and then forgot about him. The storm had wandered away into eastern Tennessee and broken against the mountains, and we were taking off in less than an hour. Sleepy-eyed travellers appeared from the hotel and I dozed a few minutes on one of those iron maidens they use for couches. Slowly the idea of a perilous journey was recreated out of the debris of our failure: a new stewardess, tall, handsome, flashing dark, exactly like the other except she wore seersucker instead of Frenchy red-and-blue, went briskly past us with a suitcase. Wylie sat beside me as we waited.

"Did you give the note to Mr. Smith?" I asked, half asleep.

"Yeah."

"Who is Mr. Smith? I suspect he spoiled Mr. Schwartze's trip."

"It was Schwartze's fault."

"I'm prejudiced against steam-rollers," I said. "My father tries to be a steam-roller around the house, and I tell him to save it for the studio."

I wondered if I was being fair; words are the palest counters at that time in the morning. "Still, he steam-rollered me into Bennington and I've always been grateful for that."

"There would be quite a crash—" Wylie said, "—if steam-roller Brady met steam-roller Smith."

"Is Mr. Smith a competitor of Father's?"

"Not exactly. I should say no. But if he was a competitor I know where my money would be."

"On Father?"

"I'm afraid not."

It was too early in the morning for family patriotism. The pilot was at the desk with the purser and he shook his head as they regarded a prospective passenger who had put two nickels in the electric phonograph and lay alcoholically on a bench fighting off sleep. The first song he had chosen, "Lost," thundered through the room, followed, after a slight interval, by his other choice, "Gone," which was equally dogmatic and final. The pilot shook his head emphatically and walked over to the passenger.

"Afraid we're not going to be able to carry you this time, old man."

"Wha?"

The drunk sat up, awful looking, yet discernibly attractive, and I was sorry for him in spite of his passionately ill-chosen music.

"Go back to the hotel and get some sleep. There'll be another plane tonight."

"Only going up in ee *air*."

"Not this time, old man."

In his disappointment the drunk fell off the bench—and above the phonograph, a loudspeaker summoned us respectable people outside. In the corridor of the plane I ran into Monroe Stahr and fell all over him, or wanted to. There was a man any girl would go for, with or without encouragement. I was emphatically with*out* it, but he liked me and sat down opposite till the plane took off.

"Let's all ask for our money back," he suggested. His dark eyes took me in, and I wondered what they would look like if he fell in love. They were kind, aloof and, though they often reasoned with you gently, somewhat superior. It was no fault of theirs if they saw so much. He darted in and out of the role of "one of the boys" with dexterity—but on the whole I should say he wasn't one of them. But he knew how to shut up, how to draw into the background, how to listen. From where he stood (and though he was not a tall man it always seemed high up) he watched the multitudinous practicalities of his world like a proud young shepherd, to whom night and day had never mattered. He was born sleepless without a talent for rest or the desire for it.

We sat in unembarrassed silence—I had known him since he became Father's partner a dozen years ago, when I was seven and Stahr was twenty-two. Wylie was across the aisle and I didn't know whether or not to introduce them, but Stahr kept turning his ring so abstractedly that he made me feel young and invisible, and I didn't dare. I never dared look quite away from him or quite *at* him, unless I had something important to say—and I knew he affected many other people in the same manner.

"I'll *give* you this ring, Cecelia."

"I beg your pardon. I didn't realize that I was—"

"I've got half a dozen like it."

He handed it to me, a gold nugget with the letter S in bold relief. I had been thinking how oddly its bulk contrasted with his fingers, which were delicate and slender like the rest of his body, and like his slender face with the arched eyebrows and the dark curly hair. He looked spiritual at times but he was a fighter—somebody out of his past knew him when he was one of a gang of kids in the Bronx, and gave me a description of how he walked always at the head of his gang, this rather frail boy, occasionally throwing a command backward out of the corner of his mouth.

Stahr folded my hand over the ring, stood up and addressed Wylie.

"Come up to the bridal suite," he said. "See you later, Cecelia."

Before they went out of hearing I heard Wylie's question, "Did you open Schwartze's note?" And Stahr:

"Not yet."

I must be slow, for only then did I realize that Stahr was Mr. Smith.

Afterwards Wylie told me what was in the note. Written by the headlights of the taxi it was almost illegible.

Dear Monro, You are the best of them all I have always admired your mentality so when you turn against me I know it's no use! I must be no good and am not going to continue the journey let me warn you once again look out! I know.

> Your friend
> MANNIE

Stahr read it twice, and raised his hand to the morning stubble on his chin.

"He's a nervous wreck," he said. "There's nothing to be done, absolutely nothing. I'm sorry I was short with him—but I don't like a man to approach me telling me it's for *my* sake."

"Maybe it was," said Wylie.

"It's poor technique."

"I'd fall for it," said Wylie. "I'm vain as a woman. If anybody pretends to be interested in me I'll ask for more. I like advice."

Stahr shook his head distastefully. Wylie kept on ribbing him—he was one of those to whom this privilege was permitted.

"You fall for some kinds of flattery," he said. "This 'little Napoleon stuff.' "

"It makes me sick," said Stahr, "but it's not as bad as some man trying to help you."

"If you don't like advice why do you pay *me*?"

"That's a question of merchandise," said Stahr. "I'm a merchant. I want to buy what's in your mind."

"You're no merchant," said Wylie. "I knew a lot of them when I was a publicity man and I agree with Charles Francis Adams."

"What did he say?"

"He knew them all—Gould, Vanderbilt, Carnegie, Astor—and he said there wasn't one he'd care to meet again in the hereafter. Well—they haven't improved since then, and that's why I say you're no merchant."

"Adams was probably a sour belly," said Stahr. "He wanted to be head man himself but he didn't have the judgement or else the character."

"He had brains," said Wylie rather tartly.

"It takes more than brains. You writers and artists poop out and get all mixed up and somebody has to come in and straighten you out." He shrugged his shoulders. "You seem to take things so personally, hating people and worshipping them—always thinking people are so important—especially yourselves. You just ask to be kicked around. I like people and I like them to like me but I wear my heart where God put it—on the inside."

He broke off.

"What did I say to Schwartze in the airport? Do you remember —exactly?"

"You said 'Whatever you're after, the answer is No.' "

Stahr was silent.

"He was sunk," said Wylie, "but I laughed him out of it. We took Pat Brady's daughter for a ride."

Stahr rang for the stewardess.

"That pilot," he said. "Would he mind if I sat up in front with him awhile?"

"That's against the rules, Mr. Smith."

"Ask him to step in here a minute when he's free."

Stahr sat up front all afternoon. While we slid off the endless desert and over the table-lands, dyed with many colors like the white sands we dyed with colors when I was a child. Then in the late afternoon, the peaks themselves—the Mountains of the Frozen Saw—slid under our propellers and we were close to home.

When I wasn't dozing I was thinking that I wanted to marry Stahr, that I wanted to make him love me. Oh, the conceit! What on earth did I have to offer? But I didn't think like that then. I had the pride of young women, which draws its strength from such sublime thoughts as "I'm as good as *she* is." For my purposes I was just as beautiful as the great beauties who must have inevitably thrown themselves at his head. My little spurt of intellectual interest was of course making me fit to be a brilliant ornament of any salon.

I know now it was absurd. Though Stahr's education was founded on nothing more than a night-school course in stenography, he had a long time ago run ahead through trackless wastes of perception into fields where very few men were able to follow him. But in my reckless conceit I matched my grey eyes against his brown ones for guile, my young golf-and-tennis heart-beats against his, which must be slowing a little after years of over-work. And I planned and I contrived and I plotted—any woman can tell you—but it never came to anything, as you will see. I still like to think that if he'd been a poor boy and nearer my age I could have managed it, but of course the real truth was that I had nothing to offer that he didn't have; some of my more romantic ideas actually stemmed from pictures—"42nd Street," for example, had a great influence on me. It's more than possible that some of the pictures which Stahr himself conceived had shaped me into what I was.

So it was rather hopeless. Emotionally, at least, people can't live by taking in each other's washing.

But at that time it was different: Father might help, the stewardess might help. She might go up in the cockpit and say to Stahr: "If I ever saw love it's in that girl's eyes."

The pilot might help: "Man are you blind? Why don't you go back there?"

Wylie White might help—instead of standing in the aisle looking at me doubtfully, wondering whether I was awake or asleep.

"Sit down," I said. "What's new, where are we?"

"Up in the air."

"Oh, so that's it. Sit down." I tried to show a cheerful interest. "What are you writing?"

"Heaven help me, I am writing about a Boy Scout—*The* Boy Scout."

"Is it Stahr's idea?"

"I don't know—he told me to look into it. He may have ten writers working ahead of me or behind me, a system which he so thoughtfully invented. So you're in love with him?"

"I should say not," I said indignantly. "I've known him all my life."

"Desperate, eh? Well, I'll arrange it if you'll use all your influence to advance me. I want a unit of my own."

I closed my eyes again and drifted off. When I woke up the stewardess was putting a blanket over me.

"Almost there," she said.

Out the window I could see by the sunset that we were in a greener land.

"I just heard something funny," she volunteered. "Up in the cockpit—that Mr. Smith—or Mr. Stahr—I never remember seeing his name."

"It's never on any pictures," I said.

"Oh. Well, he's been asking the pilots a lot about flying—I mean he's interested? You *know*?"

"I know."

"I mean one of them told me he bet he could teach Mr. Stahr solo flying in ten minutes. He has such a fine mentality, that's what he said."

I was getting impatient.

"Well, what was so funny?"

"Well, finally one of the pilots asked Mr. Smith if he liked his business and Mr. Smith said, 'Sure. Sure I like it. It's nice being the only sound nut in a hatful of cracked ones.' "

The stewardess doubled up with laughter—and I could have spit at her.

"I mean calling all those people a hatful of nuts. I mean *cracked* nuts." Her laughter stopped with unexpected suddenness and her face was grave as she stood up. "Well, I've got to finish my chart."

"Good bye."

Obviously Stahr had put the pilots right up on the throne with him and let them rule with him for a while. Years later I travelled with one of those same pilots and he told me one thing Stahr had said.

He was looking down at the mountains.

"Suppose you were a railroad man," he said. "You have to send a train through there somewhere. Well, you get your surveyors' reports, and you find there's three or four or half a dozen gaps, and not one is better than the other. You've got to decide—on what basis? You can't test the best way—except by doing it. So you just do it."

The pilot thought he had missed something.

"How do you mean?"

"You choose some one way for no reason at all—because that mountain's pink or the blueprint is a better blue. You see?"

The pilot considered that this was very valuable advice. But he doubted if he'd ever be in a position to apply it.

"What I wanted to know," he told me ruefully, "is how he ever got to be Mr. Stahr."

I'm afraid Stahr could never have answered that one, for the embryo is not equipped with a memory. But I could answer a little. He had flown up very high to see, on strong wings when he was young. And while he was up there he had looked on all the kingdoms, with the kind of eyes that can stare straight into the sun. Beating his wings tenaciously—finally frantically—and keeping on beating them he had stayed up there longer than most of us, and then, remembering all he had seen from his great height of how things were, he had settled gradually to earth.

The motors were off and all our five senses began to readjust themselves for landing. I could see a line of lights for the Long Beach Naval Station ahead and to the left, and on the right a twinkling blur for Santa Monica. The California moon was out, huge and orange over the Pacific. However I happened to feel about these things—and they were home after all—I know that Stahr must have felt much more. These were the things I had first opened my eyes on, like the sheep on the back lot of the old Laemmle studio; but this was where Stahr had come to earth after that extraordinary illuminating flight where he saw which way we were going, and how we looked doing it, and how much of it mattered. You could say that this was where an accidental wind blew him but I don't think so. I would rather think that in a "long shot" he saw a new way of measuring our jerky hopes and graceful rogueries and awkward sorrows, and that he came here from choice to be with us to the end. Like the plane coming down into the Glendale airport, into the warm darkness.

Episodes 4 and 5

It was nine o'clock of a July night and there were still some extras in the drug store across from the studio—I could see them bent over the pin-games inside—as I parked my car. "Old" Johnny Swanson stood on the corner in his semi-cowboy clothes staring gloomily past the moon. Once he had been as big in pictures as Tom Mix or Bill Hart—now it was too sad to speak to him and I hurried across the street and through the front gate.

There is never a time when a studio is absolutely quiet. There is always a night shift of technicians in the laboratories and dubbing rooms and people on the maintenance staff dropping in at the commissary. But the sounds are all different—the padded hush of tires, the quiet tick of a motor running idle, the naked cry of a soprano singing into a nightbound microphone. Around a corner I came upon a man in rubber boots washing down a car in a wonderful white light—a fountain among the dead industrial shadows. I slowed up as I saw Mr. Marcus being hoisted into his car in front of the Administration Building, because he took so long to say anything, even goodnight—and while I waited I realized that the soprano was singing "Come! Come! I love you only" over and over; I remember this because she kept singing the same line during the earthquake. That didn't come for five minutes yet.

Father's offices were in the old building with the long balconies and iron rails with their suggestion of a perpetual tightrope. Father was on the second floor with Stahr on one side and Mr. Marcus on the other—this evening there were lights all along the row. My stomach dipped a little at the proximity to Stahr but that was in pretty good control now—I'd seen him only once in the month I'd been home.

There were a lot of strange things about Father's office but I'll make it brief. In the outer part were three poker-faced secretaries who had sat there like witches ever since I could remember—Birdy Peters, Maude something, and Rosemary Schmiel; I don't know whether this was her name but she was the Dean of the trio, so to speak, and under her desk was the kick-lock that admitted you to Father's throne room. All three of the secretaries were passionate capitalists and Birdy had invented the rule that if typists were seen eating together more than once in a single week they were hauled up on the carpet. At that time the studio feared mob rule.

I went on in. Nowadays all chief executives have huge drawing rooms but my father's was the first. It was also the first to have one-way glass in the big French windows and I've heard a story about a trap in the floor that would drop unpleasant visitors to an oubliette below but believe it to be an invention. There was a big painting of Will Rogers, hung conspicuously and intended, I think, to suggest Father's essential kinship with Hollywood's St. Francis; there was a signed photograph of Minna Davis, Stahr's dead wife, and photos of other studio celebrities and big chalk drawings of Mother and me. Tonight the one-way French windows were open and a big moon, rosy-gold with a haze around, was wedged helpless in one of them. Father and Jaques La Borwits and Rosemary Schmiel were down at the end around a big circular desk.

What did Father look like? I couldn't describe him except for once in New York when I met him where I didn't expect to; I was aware of a bulky, middle-aged man who looked a little ashamed of himself and I wished he'd move on—and then I saw he was Father. Afterward I was shocked at my impression. Father can be very magnetic—he has a tough jaw and an Irish smile.

But as for Jaques La Borwits I shall spare you. Let me just say he was an assistant producer which is something like a commissar, and let it go at that. Where Stahr picked up such mental cadavers or had them forced upon him—or especially how he got any use out of them—has always amazed me, as it amazed everyone fresh from the East who slapped up against them. Jaques La Borwits had his points, no doubt, but so have the sub-microscopic protozoa, so has a dog prowling for a bitch and a bone. Jaques La—oh, my!

From their expressions I was sure they had been talking about Stahr. Stahr had ordered something or forbidden something, or defied Father or junked one of La Borwits' pictures or something catastrophic and they were sitting there in protest at night in a community of rebellion and helplessness. Rosemary Schmiel sat pad in hand as if ready to write down their dejection.

"I'm to drive you home dead or alive," I told Father. "All those birthday presents rotting away in their packages!"

"A birthday!" cried Jaques in a flurry of apology. "How old? I didn't know."

"Forty-three," said Father distinctly.

He was older than that—four years—and Jaques knew it; I saw him note it down in his account book to use sometime. Out here these account books are carried open in the hand. One can see the entries being made without recourse to lip reading and Rosemary Schmiel was compelled in emulation to make a mark on her pad. As she rubbed it out the earth quaked under us.

We didn't get the full shock like at Long Beach where the upper stories of shops were spewed into the streets and small hotels drifted out to sea—but for a full minute our bowels were one with the bowels of the earth—like some nightmare attempt to attach our navel cords again and jerk us back to the womb of creation.

Mother's picture fell off the wall revealing a small safe—Rosemary and I grabbed frantically for each other and did a strange screaming waltz across the room. Jaques fainted or at least disappeared and Father clung to his desk and shouted "Are you all right?" Outside the window the singer came to the climax of "I love you only," held it a moment and then, I swear, started it all over. Or maybe they were playing it back to her from the recording machine.

The room stood still, shimmying a little. We made our way to the door, suddenly including Jaques who had reappeared, and tottered out dizzily through the ante-room on to the iron balcony. Almost all the lights were out and from here and there we could hear cries and calls. Momentarily we stood waiting for a second shock—then as with a common impulse we went into Stahr's entry and through to his office.

The office was big but not as big as Father's. Stahr sat on the side of his couch rubbing his eyes. When the quake came he had been asleep and he wasn't sure yet whether he had dreamed it. When we convinced him he thought it was all rather funny—until the telephones began to ring. I watched him as unobtrusively as possible. He was grey with fatigue while he listened to the phone and Dictograph but as the reports came in, his eyes began to pick up shine.

"A couple of water mains have burst," he said to Father, "—they're heading into the back lot."

"Gray's shooting in the French Village," said Father.

"It's flooded around the Station too and in the Jungle and the City Corner, what the hell—nobody seems to be hurt." In passing he shook my hands gravely. "Where've you been, Cecelia?"

"You going out there, Monroe?" Father asked.

"When all the news is in. One of the power lines is off too—I've sent for Robinson."

He made me sit down with him on the couch and tell about the quake again.

"You look tired," I said, cute and motherly.

"Yes," he agreed, "I've got no place to go in the evenings so I just work."

"I'll arrange some evenings for you."

"I used to play poker with a gang," he said thoughtfully. "Before I was married. But they all drank themselves to death."

Miss Doolan, his secretary, came in with fresh bad news.

"Robby'll take care of everything when he comes," Stahr assured Father. He turned to me. "Now there's a man—that Robinson. He was a trouble-shooter—fixed the telephone wires in Minnesota blizzards—nothing stumps him. He'll be here in a minute—you'll like Robby."

He said it as if it had been his life-long intention to bring us together, and he had arranged the whole earthquake with just that in mind.

"Yes, you'll like Robby," he repeated. "When do you go back to college?"

"I've just come home."

"You get the whole summer?"

"I'm sorry," I said. "I'll go back as soon as I can."

I was in a mist. It hadn't failed to cross my mind that he might have some intention about me but if it was so, it was in an exasperatingly early stage—I was merely "a good property." And the idea didn't seem so attractive at that moment—like marrying a doctor. He seldom left the studio before eleven.

"How long—" he asked my father, "—before she graduates from college? That's what I was trying to say."

And I think I was about to sing out eagerly that I needn't go back at all, that I was quite educated already—when the totally admirable Robinson came in. He was a bowlegged young redhead, all ready to go.

"This is Robby, Cecelia," said Stahr. "Come on, Robby."

So I met Robby. I can't say it seemed like fate—but it was. For it was Robby who later told me how Stahr found his love that night.

Episode 6

Under the moon the back lot was thirty acres of fairyland—not because the locations really looked like African jungles and French châteaux and schooners at anchor and Broadway by night, but because they looked like the torn picture books of childhood, like fragments of stories dancing in an open fire. I never lived in a house with an attic but a back lot must be something like that and at night of course in an enchanted distorted way, it all comes true.

When Stahr and Robby arrived clusters of lights had already picked out the danger spots in the flood.

"We'll pump it out into the swamp on Thirty-sixth Street," said

Robby after a moment. "It's city property—but isn't this an act of God? Say—look there!"

On top of a huge head of the god Siva, two women were floating down the current of an impromptu river. The idol had come un-loosed from a set of Burma and it meandered earnestly on its way, stopping sometimes to waddle and bump in the shallows with the other debris of the tide. The two refugees had found sanctuary along a scroll of curls on its bald forehead and seemed at first glance to be sightseers on an interesting bus-ride through the scene of the flood.

"Will you look at that, Monroe!" said Robby. "Look at those dames!"

Dragging their legs through sudden bogs they made their way to the bank of the stream. Now they could see the women looking a little scared but brightening at the prospect of rescue.

"We ought to let 'em drift out to the waste pipe," said Robby gallantly, "but De Mille needs that head next week."

He wouldn't have hurt a fly though and presently he was hip deep in the water fishing for them with a pole and succeeding only in spinning it in a dizzy circle. Help arrived and the impression quickly got around that one of them was very pretty and then that they were people of importance. But they were just strays and Robby waited disgustedly to give them hell while the thing was brought finally into control and beached.

"Put that head back!" he called up to them. "You think it's a souvenir?"

One of the women came sliding smoothly down the cheek of the idol and Robby caught and set her on solid ground; the other one hesitated and then followed. Robby turned to Stahr for judgement.

"What'll we do with them, chief?"

Stahr did not answer. Smiling faintly at him from not four feet away was the face of his dead wife, identical even to the expression. Across the four feet of moonlight the eyes he knew looked back at him, a curl blew a little on a familiar forehead, the smile lingered changed a little according to pattern, the lips parted—the same. An awful fear went over him and he wanted to cry aloud. Back from the still sour room, the muffled glide of the limousine hearse, the falling concealing flowers, from out there in the dark—here now warm and glowing. The river passed him in a rush, the great spot-lights swooped and blinked—and then he heard another voice speak that was not Minna's voice.

"We're sorry," said the voice. "We followed a truck in through a gate."

A little crowd had gathered—electricians, grips, truckers—and Robby began to nip at them like a sheep dog.

". . . get the big pumps on the tanks on Stage 4 . . . put a cable around this head . . . raft it up on a couple of two-by-fours . . . get the water out of the Jungle first for Christ's sake . . . that big A pipe lay it down, all that stuff is plastic. . . ."

Stahr stood watching the two women as they threaded their way after a policeman toward an exit gate. Then he took a tentative step to see if the weakness had gone out of his knees. A loud tractor came bumping through the slush and men began streaming by him—every second one glancing at him smiling speaking Hello Monroe . . . Hello Mr. Stahr . . . wet night Mr. Stahr . . . Monroe . . . Monroe . . . Stahr . . . Stahr . . . Stahr.

He spoke and waved back as the people streamed by in the dark-ness, looking I suppose a little like the Emperor and the Old Guard. There is no world so but it has its heroes and Stahr was the hero. Most of these men had been here a long time—through the begin-nings and the great upset when sound came and the three years of Depression he had seen that no harm came to them. The old loyal-ties were trembling now—there were clay feet everywhere—but still he was their man, the last of the princes. And their greeting was a sort of low cheer as they went by.

Episode 7

Between the night I got back and the quake I'd made many observations.

About Father, for example. I loved Father—in a sort of irregular graph with many low swoops—but I began to see that his strong will didn't fill him out as a passable man. Most of what he accom-plished boiled down to shrewd. He had acquired with luck and shrewdness a quarter interest in a booming circus—together with young Stahr. That was his life's effort—all the rest was an instinct to hang on. Of course he talked that double talk to Wall Street about how mysterious it was to make a picture but Father didn't know the ABC's of dubbing or even cutting. Nor had he learned much about the feel of America as a bar boy in Ballyhegan nor have any more than a drummer's sense of a story. On the other hand he didn't have concealed paresis like ———; he came to the studio before noon, and with a suspiciousness developed like a muscle it was hard to put anything over on him.

Stahr had been his luck—and Stahr was something else again. He was a marker in industry like Edison and Lumière and Griffith and Chaplin. He led pictures way up past the range and power of the theatre, reaching a sort of golden age before the censorship in 1933. Proof of his leadership was the spying that went on around him—not just for inside information or patented process secrets—but spying on his scent for a trend in taste, his guess as how things were going to be. Too much of his vitality was taken by the mere parrying of these attempts. It made his work secret in part, often devious, slow—and hard to describe as the plans of a general—where the psychological factors become too tenuous and we end by merely adding up the successes and failures. But I have determined to give you a glimpse of him functioning, which is my excuse for what follows. It is drawn partly from a paper I wrote in college on "A Producer's Day" and partly from my imagination. More often I have blocked in the ordinary events myself, while the stranger ones are true.

In the early morning after the flood, a man walked up to the outside balcony of the Administration Building. He lingered there some time according to an eyewitness, then mounted to the iron railing and dove head first to the pavement below. Breakage—one arm.

Miss Doolan, Stahr's secretary, told him about it when he buzzed for her at nine. He had slept in his office without hearing the small commotion.

"Pete Zavras!" Stahr exclaimed, "—the camera man?"

"They took him to a doctor's office. It won't be in the paper."

"Hell of a thing," he said, "I knew he'd gone to pot—but I don't know why. He was all right when we used him two years ago—why should he come here? How did he get in?"

"He bluffed it with his old studio pass," said Catherine Doolan. She was a dry hawk, the wife of an assistant director. "Perhaps the quake had something to do with it."

"He was the best camera man in town," Stahr said. When he had heard of the thousands dead at Long Beach he was still haunted by the abortive suicide at dawn. He told Catherine Doolan to trace the matter down.

The first Dictograph messages blew in through the warm morning. While he shaved and had coffee he talked and listened. Robby had left a message: "If Mr. Stahr wants me tell him to hell with it I'm in bed." An actor was sick or thought so; the Governor of California was bringing a party out; a supervisor had beaten up his wife for the prints and must be "reduced to a writer"—these three affairs were Father's job—unless the actor was under personal contract to Stahr. There was early snow on a location in Canada with the company already there—Stahr raced over the possibilities of salvage reviewing the story of the picture. Nothing. Stahr called Catherine Doolan.

"I want to speak to the cop who put two women off the back lot last night. I think his name's Malone."

"Yes, Mr. Stahr. I've got Joe Wyman—about the trousers."

"Hello Joe," said Stahr. "Listen—two people at the sneak preview complained that Morgan's fly was open for half the picture . . . of course they're exaggerating but even if it's only ten feet . . . no, we can't find the people but I want that picture run over and over until you find that footage. Get a lot of people in the projection room—somebody'll spot it."

> *Tout passe.—L'art robuste*
> *Seul a l'éternité.*

"And there's the Prince from Denmark," said Catherine Doolan. "He's very handsome." She was impelled to add pointlessly "—for a tall man."

"Thanks," Stahr said. "Thank you, Catherine, I appreciate it that I am now the handsomest small man on the lot. Send the Prince out on the sets and tell him we'll lunch at one."

"And Mr. George Boxley—looking very angry in a British way."

"I'll see him for ten minutes."

As she went out he asked:

"Did Robby phone in?"

"No."

"Call Sound and if he's been heard from call him and ask him this. Ask him this—did he hear that woman's name last night. Either of those women. Or anything so they could be traced."

"Anything else?"

"No, but tell him it's important while he still remembers. What were they? I mean what kind of people—ask him that too. I mean were they—"

She waited, scratching his words on her pad without looking.

"—oh, were they—questionable? Were they theatrical? Never mind—skip that. Just ask if he knows how they can be traced."

The policeman, Malone, had known nothing. Two dames and he had hustled 'em you betcha. One of them was sore. Which one? One of them. They had a car, a Chevvy, he thought of taking the license. Was it—the good looker who was sore? It was one of them.

Not which one—he had noticed nothing. Even on the lot here Minna was forgotten. In three years. So much for that then.

Episode 8

Stahr smiled at Mr. George Boxley. It was a kindly fatherly smile Stahr had developed inversely when he was a young man pushed into high places. Originally it had been a smile of respect toward his elders, then as his own decisions grew rapidly to displace theirs, a smile so that they should not feel it—finally emerging as what it was, a smile of kindness sometimes a little hurried and tired but always there, toward anyone who had not angered him within the hour. Or anyone he did not intend to insult aggressive and outright.

Mr. Boxley did not smile back. He came in with the air of being violently dragged though no one apparently had a hand on him. He stood in front of a chair and again it was as if two invisible attendants seized his arms and set him down forcibly into it. He sat there morosely. Even when he lit a cigarette on Stahr's invitation one felt that the match was held to it by exterior forces he disdained to control.

Stahr looked at him courteously.

"Something not going well, Mr. Boxley?"

The novelist looked back at him in thunderous silence.

"I read your letter," said Stahr. The tone of the pleasant young headmaster was gone. He spoke as to an equal but with a faint two-edged deference.

"I can't get what I write on paper," broke out Boxley. "You've all been very decent but it's a sort of conspiracy. Those two hacks you've teamed me with listen to what I say but they spoil it—they seem to have a vocabulary of about a hundred words."

"Why don't you write it yourself?" asked Stahr.

"I have. I sent you some."

"But it was just talk, back and forth," said Stahr mildly. "Interesting talk but nothing more."

Now it was all the two ghostly attendants could do to hold Boxley in the deep chair. He struggled to get up; he uttered a single quiet bark which had some relation to laughter but none to amusement, and said:

"I don't think you people read things. The men are dueling when the conversation takes place. At the end one of them falls into a well and has to be hauled up in a bucket."

He barked again and subsided.

"Would you write that in a book of your own, Mr. Boxley?"

"What? Naturally not."

"You'd consider it too cheap."

"Movie standards are different," said Boxley hedging.

"Do you ever go to them?"

"No—almost never."

"Isn't it because people are always dueling and falling down wells?"

"Yes—and wearing strained facial expressions and talking incredible and unnatural dialogue."

"Skip the dialogue for a minute," said Stahr. "Granted your dialogue is more graceful than what these hacks can write—that's why we brought you out here. But let's imagine something that isn't either bad dialogue or jumping down a well. Has your office got a stove in it that lights with a match?"

"I think it has," said Boxley stiffly, "—but I never use it."

"Suppose you're in your office. You've been fighting duels or writing all day and you're too tired to fight or write any more. You're sitting there staring—dull, like we all get sometimes. A pretty stenographer that you've seen before comes into the room and you watch her—idly. She doesn't see you though you're very close to her. She takes off her gloves, opens her purse and dumps it out on a table—"

Stahr stood up, tossing his key-ring on his desk.

"She has two dimes and a nickle—and a cardboard match box. She leaves the nickle on the desk, puts the two dimes back into her purse and takes her black gloves to the stove, opens it and puts them inside. There is one match in the match box and she starts to light it kneeling by the stove. You notice that there's a stiff wind blowing in the window—but just then your telephone rings. The girl picks it up, says hello—listens—and says deliberately into the phone 'I've never owned a pair of black gloves in my life.' She hangs up, kneels by the stove again, and just as she lights the match you glance around very suddenly and see that there's another man in the office, watching every move the girl makes—"

Stahr paused. He picked up his keys and put them in his pocket.

"Go on," said Boxley smiling. "What happens?"

"I don't know," said Stahr. "I was just making pictures."

Boxley felt he was being put in the wrong.

"It's just melodrama," he said.

"Not necessarily," said Stahr. "In any case nobody has moved violently or talked cheap dialogue or had any facial expression at all. There was only one bad line, and a writer like you could improve it. But you were interested."

"What was the nickle for?" asked Boxley evasively.

"I don't know," said Stahr. Suddenly he laughed, "Oh yes—the nickle was for the movies."

The two invisible attendants seemed to release Boxley. He relaxed, leaned back in his chair and laughed.

"What in hell do you pay me for?" he demanded. "I don't understand the damn stuff."

"You will," said Stahr grinning. "Or you wouldn't have asked about the nickle."

A dark saucer-eyed man was waiting in the outer office as they came out.

"Mr. Boxley, this is Mr. Mike Van Dyke," Stahr said. "What is it, Mike?"

"Nothing," Mike said. "I just came up to see if you were real."

"Why don't you go to work?" Stahr said. "I haven't had a laugh in the rushes for days."

"I'm afraid of a nervous breakdown."

"You ought to keep in form," Stahr said. "Let's see you peddle your stuff." He turned to Boxley. "Mike's a gag man—he was out here when I was in the cradle. Mike, show Mr. Boxley a double wing, clutch, kick and scram."

"Here?" asked Mike.

"Here."

"There isn't much room. I wanted to ask you about—"

"There's lots of room."

"Well," he looked around tentatively. "You shoot the gun."

Miss Doolan's assistant, Katie, took a paper bag, blew it open.

"It was a routine," Mike said to Boxley—"back in the Keystone days." He turned to Stahr. "Does he know what a routine is?"

"It means an act," Stahr explained. "Georgie Jessel talks about 'Lincoln's Gettysburg routine.' "

Katie poised the neck of the blown up bag in her mouth. Mike stood with his back to her.

"Ready?" Katie asked. She brought her hand down on the side. Immediately Mike grabbed his bottom with both hands, jumped in the air, slid his feet out on the floor one after the other, remaining in place and flapping his arms twice like a bird—

"Double wing," said Stahr.

—And then ran—out the screen door which the office boy held open for him and disappeared past the window of the balcony.

"Mr. Stahr," said Miss Doolan, "Mr. Hanson is on the phone from New York."

Ten minutes later he clicked his Dictograph and Miss Doolan came in. There was a male star waiting to see him in the outer office Miss Doolan said.

"Tell him I went out by the balcony," Stahr advised her.

"All right. He's been in four times this week. He seems very anxious."

"Did he give you any hint of what he wanted? Isn't it something he can see Mr. Brady about?"

"He didn't say. You have a conference coming up. Miss Meloney and Mr. White are outside. Mr. Broaca is next door in Mr. Rienmund's office."

"Send ———— in," said Stahr. "Tell him I can see him only for a minute."

When the handsome actor came in Stahr remained standing.

"What is it that can't wait?" he asked pleasantly.

The actor waited carefully till Miss Doolan had gone out.

"Monroe, I'm through," he said. "I had to see you."

"Through!" said Stahr. "Have you seen 'Variety'? Your picture's held over at Roxy's and did thirty-seven thousand in Chicago last week."

"That's the worst of it. That's the tragedy. I get everything I want and now it means nothing."

"Well, go on explain."

"There's nothing between Esther and me anymore. There never can be again."

"A row."

"Oh, no—worse—I can't bear to mention it. My head's in a daze. I wander around like a madman. I go through my part as if I was asleep."

"I haven't noticed it," said Stahr. "You were great in your rushes yesterday."

"Was I? That just shows you nobody ever guesses."

"Are you trying to tell me that you and Esther are separating?"

"I suppose it'll come to that. Yes—inevitably—it will."

"What was it?" demanded Stahr impatiently. "Did she come in without knocking?"

"Oh, there's nobody else. It's just—me. I'm through."

Stahr got it suddenly.

"How do you know?"

"It's been true for six weeks."

"It's your imagination," said Stahr. "Have you been to a doctor?"

The actor nodded.

"I've tried everything. I even—one day in desperation I went down to—to Claris. But it was hopeless. I'm washed up."

Stahr had an impish temptation to tell him to go to Brady about it. Brady handled all matters of public relations. Or was this private relations. He turned away a moment, got his face in control, turned back.

"I've been to Pat Brady," said the star, as if guessing the thought. "He gave me a lot of phoney advice and I tried it all but nothing doing. Esther and I sit opposite each other at dinner and I'm ashamed to look at her. She's been a good sport about it but I'm ashamed. I'm ashamed all day long. I think 'Rainy Day' grossed 25,000 in Des Moines and broke all records in St. Louis and did 27,000 in Kansas City. My fan mail's way up and there I am afraid to go home at night, afraid to go to bed."

Stahr began to be faintly oppressed. When the actor first came in Stahr had intended to invite him to a cocktail party but now it scarcely seemed appropriate. What would he want with a cocktail party with this hanging over him. In his mind's eye he saw him wandering haunted from guest to guest with a cocktail in his hand and his grosses up 28,000.

"So I came to you, Monroe. I never saw a situation where you didn't know a way out. I said to myself even if he advises me to kill myself I'll ask Monroe."

The buzzer sounded on Stahr's desk—he switched on the Dictograph and heard Miss Doolan's voice.

"Five minutes, Mr. Stahr."

"I'm sorry," said Stahr, "I'll need a few minutes more."

"Five hundred girls marched to my house from the high school," the actor said gloomily. "And I stood behind the curtains and watched them. I couldn't go out."

"You sit down," said Stahr. "We'll take plenty of time and talk this over."

In the outer office two members of the conference group had already waited ten minutes—Wylie White and Rose Meloney. The latter was a dried up little blonde of fifty about whom one could hear the fifty assorted opinions of Hollywood—"a sentimental dope," "the best writer on construction in Hollywood," "a veteran," "that old hack," "the smartest woman on the lot," "the cleverest plagiarist in the biz," and of course in addition a nymphomaniac, a virgin, a pushover, a lesbian and a faithful wife. Without being an old maid she was like most self-made women rather old maidish. She had ulcers of the stomach and her salary was over a hundred thousand a year. A complicated treatise could be written on whether she was "worth it" or more than that or nothing at all. Her value lay in such ordinary assets as the bare fact that she was a woman and adaptable, quick and trustworthy, "knew the game" and was without egotism. She had been a great friend of Minna's and over a period of years he had managed to stifle what amounted to a sharp physical revulsion.

She and Wylie waited in silence—occasionally addressing a remark to Miss Doolan. Every few minutes Rienmund the supervisor called up from his office where he and Broaca the director were waiting. After ten minutes Stahr's button went on and Miss Doolan called Rienmund and Broaca; simultaneously Stahr and the actor came out of Stahr's office with Stahr holding the man's arm. He was so wound up now that when Wylie White asked him how he was he opened his mouth and began to tell him then and there.

"Oh, I've had an awful time," he said but Stahr interrupted sharply.

"No you haven't. Now you go along and do the role the way I said."

"Thank you, Monroe."

Rose Meloney looked after him without speaking.

"Somebody been catching flies on him?" she asked, a phrase for stealing scenes.

"I'm sorry I kept you waiting," Stahr said. "Come on in."

Episode 9

It was noon already and the conferees were entitled to exactly an hour of Stahr's time. No less, for such a conference could only be interrupted by a director who was held up in his shooting; seldom much more because every eight days the company must release a production as complex and costly as Reinhardt's "Miracle."

Occasionally, less often than five years ago, Stahr would work all through the night on a single picture. But after such a spree he felt bad for days. If he could go from problem to problem there was a certain rebirth of vitality with each change. And like those sleepers who can wake whenever they wish, he had set his psychological clock to run one hour.

The cast assembled included besides the writers Rienmund, one of the most favored of the supervisors, and John Broaca, the picture's director.

Broaca, on the surface, was an engineer—large and without nerves, quietly resolute, popular. He was an ignoramus and Stahr often caught him making the same scenes over and over—one scene about a rich young girl occurred in all his pictures with the same action, the same business. A bunch of large dogs entered the room and jumped around the girl. Later the girl went to a stable and slapped a horse on the rump. The explanation was probably not Freudian; more likely that at a drab moment in youth he had looked through a fence and seen a beautiful girl with dogs and horses. As a trademark for glamor it was stamped on his brain forever.

Rienmund was a handsome young opportunist, with a fairly good education. Originally a man of some character he was being daily forced by his anomalous position into devious ways of acting and thinking. He was a bad man now, as men go. At thirty he had none of the virtues which either native Americans or Jews are taught to think admirable. But he got his pictures out in time and by manifesting an almost homosexual fixation on Stahr, seemed to have dulled Stahr's usual acuteness. Stahr liked him—considered him a good all around man.

Wylie White, of course, would have been recognizable in any country as an intellectual of the second order. He was civilized and voluble, both simple and acute, half dazed half saturnine. His jealousy of Stahr showed only in unguarded flashes, and was mingled with admiration and even affection.

"The production date for this picture is two weeks from Saturday," said Stahr. "I think basically it's all right—much improved."

Rienmund and the two writers exchanged a glance of congratulation.

"Except for one thing," said Stahr, thoughtfully. "I don't see why it should be produced at all and I've decided to put it away."

There was a moment of shocked silence—and then murmurs of protest, stricken queries.

"It's not your fault," Stahr said. "I thought there was something there that wasn't there—that was all." He hesitated, looking regretfully at Rienmund. "It's too bad—it was a good play. We paid fifty thousand for it."

"What's the matter with it, Monroe?" asked Broaca bluntly.

"Well, it hardly seems worth while to go into it," said Stahr.

Rienmund and Wylie White were both thinking of the professional effect on them. Rienmund had two pictures to his account this year—but Wylie White needed a credit to start his comeback to the scene. Rose Meloney was watching Stahr closely from little skull-like eyes.

"Couldn't you give us some clue?" Rienmund asked. "This is a good deal of a blow, Monroe."

"I just wouldn't put Margaret Sullavan in it," said Stahr. "Or Colman either. I wouldn't advise them to play it—"

"Specifically, Monroe," begged Wylie White. "What didn't you like? The scenes? the dialogue? the humor? construction?"

Stahr picked up the script from his desk, let it fall as if it were physically too heavy to handle.

"I don't like the people," he said. "I wouldn't like to meet them—if I knew they were going to be somewhere I'd go somewhere else."

Rienmund smiled but there was worry in his eyes.

"Well, that's a damning criticism," he said. "I thought the people were rather interesting."

"So did I," said Broaca. "I thought Em was very sympathetic."

"Did you?" asked Stahr sharply. "I could just barely believe she was alive. And when I came to the end I said to myself 'So what?' "

"There must be something to do," Rienmund said. "Naturally we feel bad about this. This is the structure we agreed on—"

"But it's not the story," said Stahr. "I've told you many times that the first thing I decide is the *kind* of story I want. We change in every other regard but once that is set we've got to work toward it with every line and movement. This is not the kind of a story I want. The story we bought had shine and glow—it was a happy story. This is all full of doubt and hesitation. The hero and heroine stop loving each other over trifles—then they start up again over trifles. After the first sequence you don't care if she never sees him again or he her."

"That's my fault," said Wylie suddenly. "You see, Monroe, I don't think stenographers have the same dumb admiration for their bosses they had in 1929. They've been laid off—they've seen their bosses jittery. The world has moved on, that's all."

Stahr looked at him impatiently, gave a short nod.

"That's not under discussion," he said. "The premise of this story is that the girl did have dumb admiration for her boss if you want to call it that. And there wasn't any evidence that he'd ever been jittery. When you make her doubt him in any way you have a different kind of story. Or rather you haven't anything at all. These people are extraverts—get that straight—and I want them to extravert all over the lot. When I want to do a Eugene O'Neill play I'll buy one."

Rose Meloney who had never taken her eyes off Stahr knew it was going to be all right now. If he had really been going to abandon the picture he wouldn't have gone at it like this. She had been in this game longer than any of them except Broaca with whom she had had a three day affair twenty years ago.

Stahr turned to Rienmund.

"You ought to have understood from the casting, Rieny, what kind of a picture I wanted. I started marking the lines that Carroll and MacMurray couldn't say and got tired of it. Remember this in future—if I order a limousine I want that kind of car. And the fastest midget racer you ever saw wouldn't do. Now—" He looked around. "Shall we go any farther? Now that I've told you I don't even like the kind of picture this is? Shall we go on? We've got two weeks. At the end of that time I'm going to put Carroll and Mac-Murray into this or something else—is it worth while?"

"Well naturally," said Rienmund, "I think it is. I feel bad about this. I should have warned Wylie. I thought he had some good ideas."

"Monroe's right," said Broaca bluntly. "I felt this was wrong all the time but I couldn't put my finger on it."

Wylie and Rose looked at him contemptuously and exchanged a glance.

"Do you writers think you can get hot on it again?" asked Stahr, not unkindly. "Or shall I try somebody fresh?"

"I'd like another shot," said Wylie.

"How about you, Rose?"

She nodded briefly.

"What do you think of the girl?" asked Stahr.

"Well—naturally I'm prejudiced in her favor."

"You better forget it," said Stahr warningly. "Ten million Americans would put thumbs down on that girl if she walked on the screen. We've got an hour and twenty-five minutes on the screen—you show a woman being unfaithful to a man for one-third of that time and you've given the impression that she's one-third whore."

"Is that a big proportion?" asked Rose slyly, and they laughed.

"It is for me," said Stahr thoughtfully, "even if it wasn't for the

Hays office. If you want to paint a scarlet letter on her back it's all right but that's another story. Not this story. This is a future wife and mother. However—*however*—"

He pointed his pencil at Wylie White.

"—this has as much passion as that Oscar on my desk."

"What the hell!" said Wylie. "She's full of it. Why she goes to—"

"She's loose enough," said Stahr, "—but that's all. There's one scene in the play better than all this you cooked up and you've left it out. When she's trying to make the time pass by changing her watch."

"It didn't seem to fit," Wylie apologized.

"Now," said Stahr, "I've got about fifty ideas. I'm going to call Miss Doolan." He pressed a button. "—and if there's anything you don't understand speak up—"

Miss Doolan slid in almost imperceptibly. Pacing the floor swiftly Stahr began. In the first place he wanted to tell them what kind of a girl she was—what kind of a girl he approved of here. She was a perfect girl with a few small faults as in the play but a perfect girl not because the public wanted her that way but because it was the kind of girl that he, Stahr, liked to see in this sort of picture. Was that clear? It was no character role. She stood for health, vitality, ambition and love. What gave the play its importance was entirely a situation in which she found herself. She became possessed of a secret that affected a great many lives. There was a right thing and a wrong thing to do—at first it was not plain which was which but when it was she went right away and did it. That was the kind of story this was—thin, clean and shining. No doubts.

"She has never heard the word labor troubles," he said with a sigh. "She might be living in 1929. Is it plain what kind of girl I want?"

"It's very plain, Monroe."

"Now about the things she does," said Stahr. "At all times, at all moments when she is on the screen in our sight she wants to sleep with Ken Willard. Is that plain, Wylie?"

"Passionately plain."

"Whatever she does it is in place of sleeping with Ken Willard. If she walks down the street she is walking to sleep with Ken Willard, if she eats her food it is to give her strength to sleep with Ken Willard. *But* at no time do you give the impression that she would ever consider sleeping with Ken Willard unless they were properly sanctified. I'm ashamed of having to tell you these kindergarten facts but they have somehow leaked out of the story."

He opened the script and began to go through it page by page. Miss Doolan's notes would be typed in quintuplicate and given to them but Rose Meloney made notes of her own. Broaca put his hand up to his half closed eyes—he could remember "when a director was something out here," when writers were gag men or eager and ashamed young reporters full of whiskey—a director was all there was then. No supervisor—no Stahr.

He started wide awake as he heard his name.

"It would be nice, John, if you could put the boy on a pointed roof and let him walk around and keep the camera on him. You might get a nice feeling—not danger, not suspense, not pointing for anything—a kid on the roof in the morning."

Broaca brought himself back in the room.

"All right," he said. "—just an element of danger."

"Not exactly," said Stahr. "He doesn't start to fall off the roof. Break into the next scene with it."

"Through the window," suggested Rose Meloney. "He could climb in his sister's window."

"That's a good transition," said Stahr. "Right into the diary scene."

Broaca was wide awake now.

"I'll shoot up at him," he said. "Let him go away from the camera. Just a fixed shot from quite a distance—let him go away from the camera. Don't follow him. Pick him up in a close shot and let him go away again. No attention on him except against the whole roof and the sky." He liked the shot—it was a director's shot that didn't come up on every page any more. He might use a crane—it would be cheaper in the end than building the roof on the ground with a process sky. That was one thing about Stahr—the literal sky was the limit. He had worked with Jews too long to believe legends that they were small with money.

"In the third sequence have him hit the priest," Stahr said.

"What!" Wylie cried, "—and have the Catholics on our neck."

"I've talked to Joe Breen. Priests have been hit. It doesn't reflect on them."

His quiet voice ran on—stopped abruptly as Miss Doolan glanced at the clock.

"Is that too much to do before Monday?" he asked Wylie.

Wylie looked at Rose and she looked back not even bothering to nod. He saw their week-end melting away, but he was a different man from when he entered the room. When you were paid fifteen hundred a week emergency work was one thing you did not skimp, nor when your picture was threatened. As a "free lance" writer Wylie had failed from lack of caring but here was Stahr to care, for all of them. The effect would not wear off when he left the office—not anywhere within the walls of the lot. He felt a great purposefulness. The mixture of common sense, wise sensibility, theatrical ingenuity, and a certain half naive conception of the common weal which Stahr had just stated aloud, inspired him to do his part, to get his block of stone in place, even if the effort were foredoomed, the result as dull as a pyramid.

Out the window Rose Meloney watched the trickle streaming toward the commissary. She would have her lunch in her office and knit a few rows while it came. The man was coming at one-fifteen with the French perfume smuggled over the Mexican border. That was no sin—it was like prohibition.

Broaca watched as Rienmund fawned upon Stahr. He sensed that Rienmund was on his way up—not yet. He received seven hundred and fifty a week for his partial authority over directors, writers and stars who got much more. He wore a cheap English shoe he bought near the Beverly Wilshire and Broaca hoped they hurt his feet, but soon now he would order his shoes from Peal's and put away his little green alpine hat with a feather. Broaca was years ahead of him. He had a fine record in the war but he had never felt quite the same with himself since he had let Ike Franklin strike him in the face with his open hand.

There was smoke in the room and behind it, behind his great desk Stahr was withdrawing further and further, in all courtesy, still giving Rienmund an ear and Miss Doolan an ear. The conference was over.

"Any messages?"

"Mr. Robinson called in," Miss Doolan said, as he started for the commissary. "One of the women told him her name but he's forgotten it—he thinks it was Smith or Brown or Jones."

"That's a great help."

"And he remembers she says she just moved to Los Angeles."

"I remember she had a silver belt," Stahr said, "with stars cut out of it."

"I'm still trying to find out more about Pete Zavras. I talked to his wife."

"What did she say?"

"Oh, they've had an awful time—given up their house—she's been sick—"

"Is the eye trouble hopeless?"

"She didn't seem to know anything about the state of his eyes. She didn't even know he was going blind."

"That's funny."

He thought about it on the way to luncheon but it was as confusing as the actor's trouble this morning. Troubles about people's health didn't seem within his range—he gave no thought to his own. In the lane beside the commissary he stepped back as an open electric truck crammed with girls in the bright costumes of the regency came rolling in from the back lot. The dresses were fluttering in the wind, the young painted faces looked at him curiously and he smiled as it went by.

Episode 10

Eleven men and their guest Prince Agge sat at lunch in the private dining room of the studio commissary. They were the money men—they were the rulers and unless there was a guest they ate in broken silence, sometimes asking questions about each other's wives and children, sometimes discharging a single absorption from the forefront of their consciousness. Eight out of the ten were Jews—five of the ten were foreign born, including a Greek and an Englishman—and they had all known each other for a long time: there was a rating in the group, from old Marcus down to old Leanbaum who had bought the most fortunate block of stock in the business and never was allowed to spend over a million a year producing.

Old Marcus functioned with disquieting resilience. Some never-atrophying instinct warned him of danger, of gangings up against him—he was never so dangerous himself as when others considered him surrounded. His grey face had attained such immobility that even those who were accustomed to watch the reflex of the inner corner of his eye could no longer see it—nature had grown a little white whisker there to conceal it; his armor was complete.

As he was the oldest, Stahr was the youngest of the group—not by many years at this date, though he had first sat with most of these men when he was a boy wonder of twenty-two. Then, more than now, he had been a money man among money men. Then he had been able to figure costs in his head with a speed and accuracy that dazzled them—for they were not wizards or even experts in that regard, despite the popular conception of Jews in finance. Most of them owed their success to different and incompatible qualities. But in a group a tradition carries along the less adept, and they were content to look at Stahr for the sublimated auditing and experience a sort of glow as if they had done it themselves like rooters at a football game.

Stahr, as will presently be seen, had grown away from that particular gift, though it was always there.

Prince Agge sat between Stahr and Mort Flieshacker the company lawyer and across from Joe Popolous the theatre owner. He was hostile to Jews in a vague general way that he tried to cure himself of. As a turbulent man, serving his time in the Foreign Legion, he thought that Jews were too fond of their own skins. But he was willing to concede that they might be different in America under different circumstances, and certainly he found Stahr was much of a man in every way. For the rest—he thought most business men were dull dogs—for final reference he reverted always to the blood of Bernadotte in his veins.

My father—I will call him Mr. Brady as Prince Agge did when he told me of this luncheon—was worried about a picture and when Leanbaum went out early he came up and took his chair opposite.

"How about the South America picture idea, Monroe?" he asked.

Prince Agge noticed a blink of attention toward them as distinct as if a dozen pair of eyelashes had made the sound of batting wings. Then silence again.

"We're going ahead with it," said Stahr.

"With that same budget?" Brady asked.

Stahr nodded.

"It's out of proportion," said Brady. "There won't be any miracle in these bad times—no 'Hell's Angels' or 'Ben-Hur' when you throw it away and get it back."

Probably the attack was planned, for Popolous, the Greek, took up the matter in a sort of double talk that reminded Prince Agge of Mike Van Dyke except that it tried to be and succeeded in being clear instead of confusing.

"It's not adoptable, Monroe, in as we wish adopt to this times in as it changes. It what could be done as we run the gamut of prosperity is scarcely conceptuable now."

"What do you think, Mr. Marcus?" asked Stahr.

All eyes followed his down the table but as if forewarned Mr. Marcus had already signalled his private waiter behind him that he wished to rise, and was even now in a basket-like position in the waiter's arms. He looked at them with such helplessness that it was hard to realize that in the evenings he sometimes went dancing with his young Canadian girl.

"Monroe is our production genius," he said. "I count upon Monroe and lean heavily upon him. I have not seen the flood myself."

There was a moment of silence as he moved from the room.

"There's not a two million dollar gross in the country now," said Brady.

"Is not," agreed Popolous. "Even as if so you could grab them by the head and push them by and in, is not."

"Probably not," agreed Stahr. He paused as if to make sure that all were listening. "I think we can count on a million and a quarter from the road-show. Perhaps a million and a half altogether. And a quarter of a million abroad."

Again there was silence—this time puzzled, a little confused. Over his shoulder Stahr asked the waiter to be connected with his office on the phone.

"But your budget?" said Flieshacker. "Your budget is seventeen hundred and fifty thousand, I understand. And your expectations only add up to that without profit."

"Those aren't my expectations," said Stahr. "We're not sure of more than a million and a half."

The room had grown so motionless that Prince Agge could hear a grey chunk of ash fall from a cigar in midair. Flieshacker started to speak, his face fixed with amazement, but a phone had been handed over Stahr's shoulder.

"Your office, Mr. Stahr."

"Oh yes—oh, hello Miss Doolan. I've figured it out about Zavras. It's one of these lousy rumors—I'll bet my shirt on it. . . . Oh, you did. Good. . . . Good. Now here's what to do—send him to my oculist this afternoon, Dr. John Kennedy, and have him get a report and have it photostated—you understand."

He hung up—turned with a touch of passion to the table at large.

"Did any of you ever hear a story that Pete Zavras was going blind?"

There were a couple of nods. But most of those present were poised breathlessly on whether Stahr had slipped on his figures a minute before.

"It's pure bunk. He says he's never even been to an oculist—never knew why the studios turned against him," said Stahr. "Somebody didn't like him or somebody talked too much and he's been out of work for a year."

There was a conventional murmur of sympathy. Stahr signed the check and made as though to get up.

"Excuse me, Monroe," said Flieshacker persistently, while Brady and Popolous watched, "I'm fairly new here and perhaps I fail to comprehend implicitly and explicitly." He was talking fast but the veins on his forehead bulged with pride at the big words from

N.Y.U. "Do I understand you to say you expect to gross a quarter million short of your budget?"

"It's a quality picture," said Stahr with assumed innocence.

It had dawned on them all now but they still felt there was a trick in it. Stahr really thought it would make money. No one in his senses—

"For two years we've played safe," said Stahr. "It's time we made a picture that'll lose some money. Write it off as good will—this'll bring in new customers."

Some of them still thought he meant it was a flyer and a favorable one but he left them in no doubt.

"It'll lose money," he said as he stood up, his jaw just slightly out and his eyes smiling and shining. "It would be a bigger miracle than 'Hell's Angels' if it broke even. But we have a certain duty to the public as Pat Brady says at Academy dinners. It's a good thing for the production schedule to slip in a picture that'll lose money."

He nodded at Prince Agge. As the latter made his bows quickly he tried to take in with a last glance the general effect of what Stahr said, but he could tell nothing. The eyes not so much downcast as fixed upon an indefinite distance just above the table were all blinking quickly now but there was not a whisper in the room.

Coming out of the private dining room they passed through a corner of the commissary proper. Prince Agge drank it in—eagerly. It was gay with gypsies and with citizens and soldiers with the sideburns and braided coats of the First Empire. From a little distance they were men who lived and walked a hundred years ago and Agge wondered how he and the men of his time would look as extras in some future costume picture.

Then he saw Abraham Lincoln and his whole feeling suddenly changed. He had been brought up in the dawn of Scandanavian socialism where Nicolay's biography was much read. He had been told Lincoln was a great man whom he should admire and he had hated him instead because he was forced upon him. But now seeing him sitting here, his legs crossed, his kindly face fixed on a forty cent dinner, including dessert, his shawl wrapped around him as if to protect himself from the erratic air-cooling—now Prince Agge, who was in America at last, stared as a tourist at the mummy of Lenin in the Kremlin. This then was Lincoln. Stahr had walked on far ahead of him, turned waiting for him—but still Agge stared.

—This then, he thought, was what they all meant to be.

Lincoln suddenly raised a triangle of pie and jammed it in his mouth and, a little frightened, Prince Agge hurried to join Stahr.

"I hope you're getting what you want," said Stahr feeling he had neglected him. "We'll have some rushes in half an hour and then you can go on to as many sets as you want."

"I should rather stay with you," said Prince Agge.

"I'll see what there is for me," said Stahr. "Then we'll go on together."

There was the Japanese consul on the release of a spy story which might offend the national sensibilities of Japan. There were phone calls and telegrams. There was some further information from Robby.

"Now he remembers the name of the woman was Smith," said Miss Doolan. "He asked her if she wanted to come on the lot and get some dry shoes and she said no—so she can't sue."

"That's pretty bad for a total recall—'Smith.' That's a great help." He thought a moment. "Ask the phone company for a list of Smiths that have taken new phones here in the last month. Call them all."

"All right."

For Episode 11

"How you, Monroe," said Red Ridingwood. "I'm glad you came down."

Stahr walked past him, heading across the great stage toward a set that would be used tomorrow. Director Ridingwood followed, realizing suddenly that Stahr walked a step or two ahead. He recognized the indication of displeasure—his own metier was largely the "delivery" of situations through mimetic business. He didn't know what the trouble was but he was a top director and not alarmed. Goldwyn had once interfered with him, and Ridingwood had led Goldwyn into trying to act out a part in front of fifty actors—with the result that he anticipated. His own authority had been restored.

Stahr reached the set and stared at it.

"It's no good," said Ridingwood. "I don't care how you light it—"

"Why did you call me about it?" Stahr asked standing close to him. "Why didn't you take it up with Art?"

"I didn't ask you to come down, Monroe."

"You wanted to be your own supervisor."

"I'm sorry, Monroe," said Ridingwood patiently. "But I didn't ask you to come down."

Stahr turned suddenly and walked back toward the camera set up. The eyes and open mouths of a group of visitors moved momentarily off the heroine of the picture, took in Stahr and then moved vacantly back to the heroine again. They were Knights of Columbus. They had seen the Host carried in procession but this was the dream made flesh.

Stahr stopped beside her chair. She wore a low gown which displayed the bright eczema of her chest and back. Before each take the blemished surface was plastered over with an emollient, which was removed immediately after the take. Her hair was of the color and viscosity of drying blood but there was starlight that actually photographed in her eyes.

Before Stahr could speak he heard a helpful voice behind him:

"She's radiunt. Absolutely radiunt."

It was an assistant director and the intention was delicate compliment. The actress was being complimented so that she did not have to strain her poor skin to bend and hear. Stahr was being complimented for having her under contract. Ridingwood was being remotely complimented.

"Everything all right?" Stahr asked her pleasantly.

"Oh, it's fine," she agreed, "—except for the ——ing publicity men."

He winked at her gently.

"We'll keep them away," he said.

Her name had become currently synonymous with the expression "bitch." Presumably she had modelled herself after one of those queens in the Tarzan comics who rule mysteriously over a nation of blacks. She regarded the rest of the world as black. She was a necessary evil, borrowed for a single picture.

Ridingwood walked with Stahr toward the door of the stage.

"Everything's all right," the director said. "She's as good as she can be."

They were out of hearing range and Stahr stopped suddenly and looked at Red with blazing eyes.

"You've been photographing crap," he said. "Do you know what she reminds me of in the rushes—'Miss Foodstuffs.' "

"I'm trying to get the best performance—"

"Come along with me," said Stahr abruptly.

"With you? Shall I tell them to rest?"

"Leave it as it is," said Stahr, pushing the padded outer door.

His car and chauffeur waited outside. Minutes were precious most days.

"Get in," said Stahr.

Red knew now it was serious. He even knew all at once what was the matter. The girl had got the whip hand on him the first day with her cold lashing tongue. He was a peace-loving man and he had let her walk through her part cold rather than cause trouble.

Stahr spoke into his thoughts.

"You can't handle her," he said. "I told you what I wanted. I wanted her *mean*—and she comes out bored. I'm afraid we'll have to call it off, Red."

"The picture?"

"No. I'm putting Harley on it."

"All right, Monroe."

"I'm sorry, Red. We'll try something else another time."

The car drew up in front of Stahr's office.

"Shall I finish this take?" said Red.

"It's being done now," said Stahr grimly. "Harley's in there."

"What the hell—"

"He went in when we came out. I had him read the script last night."

"Now listen, Monroe—"

"It's my busy day, Red," said Stahr tersely. "You lost interest about three days ago."

It was a sorry mess Ridingwood thought. It meant he would have to do the next picture he was offered whether he liked it or not. It meant a slight, very slight loss of position—it probably meant that he could not have a third wife just now as he had planned. There wasn't even the satisfaction in raising a row about it—if you disagreed with Stahr you did not advertise it. Stahr was his world's great customer who was always—almost always right.

"How about my coat?" he asked suddenly. "I left it over a chair on the set."

"I know you did," said Stahr. "Here it is."

He was trying so hard to be charitable about Ridingwood's lapse that he had forgotten that he had it in his hand.

Episode 11

"Mr. Stahr's Projection Room" was a miniature picture theatre with four rows of overstuffed chairs. In front of the front row ran long tables with dim lamps, buzzers and telephones. Against the wall was an upright piano, left there since the early days of sound. The room had been redecorated and reupholstered only a year before but already it was ragged again with work and hours.

Here Stahr sat at two-thirty and again at six-thirty watching the lengths of film taken during the day. There was often a savage tensity about the occasion—he was dealing with *faits accomplis*—the net result of months of buying, planning, writing and rewriting, casting, constructing, lighting, rehearsing and shooting—the fruit alike of brilliant hunches or counsels of despair, of lethargy, conspiracy and sweat. At this point the tortuous manoeuvre was staged and in suspension—these were reports from the battle-line.

Besides Stahr there were present the representatives of all technical departments together with the supervisors and unit managers of the pictures concerned. The directors did not appear at these showings—officially because their work was considered done—actually because few punches were pulled here as money ran out in silver spools. There had evolved a delicate staying away.

The staff was already assembled. Stahr came in and took his place quickly and the murmur of conversation died away. As he sat back and drew his thin knee up beside him in the chair the lights in the room went out. There was the flare of a match in the back row—then silence.

On the screen a troop of French Canadians pushed their canoes up a rapids. The scene had been photographed in a studio tank and at the end of each take after the director's voice could be heard saying "Cut," the actors on the screen relaxed and wiped their brows and sometimes laughed hilariously—and the water in the tank stopped flowing and the illusion ceased. Except to name his choice from each set of takes and to remark that it was "a good process," Stahr made no comment.

The next scene, still in the rapids, called for dialogue between the Canadian girl (Claudette Colbert) and the *coureur du bois* (Ronald Colman) with her looking down at him from a canoe. After a few strips had run through Stahr spoke up suddenly.

"Has the tank been dismantled?"

"Yes, sir."

"Monroe—they needed it for—"

Stahr cut in peremptorily.

"Have it set up again right away. Let's have that second take again."

The lights went on momentarily. One of the unit managers left his chair and came and stood in front of Stahr.

"A beautifully acted scene thrown away," raged Stahr quietly. "It wasn't centered. The camera was set up so it caught the beautiful top of Claudette's head all the time she was talking. That's just what we want, isn't it? That's just what people go to see—the top of a beautiful girl's head. Tell Tim he could have saved wear and tear by using her stand-in."

The lights went out again. The unit manager squatted by Stahr's chair to be out of the way. The take was run again.

"Do you see now?" asked Stahr. "And there's a hair in the

picture—there on the right, see it? Find out if it's in the projector or the film."

At the very end of the take Claudette Colbert slowly lifted her head revealing her great liquid eyes.

"That's what we should have had all the way," said Stahr. "She gave a fine performance too. See if you can fit it in tomorrow or late this afternoon."

—Pete Zavras would not have made a slip like that. There were not six camera men in the industry you could entirely trust.

The lights went on; the supervisor and unit manager for that picture went out.

"Monroe, this stuff was shot yesterday—it came through late last night."

The room darkened. On the screen appeared the head of Siva, immense and imperturbable, oblivious to the fact that in a few hours it was to be washed away in a flood. Around it milled a crowd of the faithful.

"When you take that scene again," said Stahr suddenly, "put a couple of little kids up on top. You better check about whether it's reverent or not but I think it's all right. Kids'll do anything."

"Yes, Monroe."

A silver belt with stars cut out of it. . . . Smith, Jones or Brown. . . . Personal—will the woman with the silver belt who—?

With another picture the scene shifted to New York, a gangster story, and suddenly Stahr became restive.

"That scene's trash," he called suddenly in the darkness. "It's badly written, it's miscast, it accomplishes nothing. Those types aren't tough. They look like a lot of dressed up lollypops—what the hell is the matter, Mort?"

"The scene was written on the set this morning," said Mort Flieshacker. "Burton wanted to get all the stuff on Stage 6."

"Well—it's trash. And so is this one. There's no use printing stuff like that. She doesn't believe what she's saying—neither does Cary. 'I love you' in a close-up—they'll cluck you out of the house! And the girl's overdressed."

In the darkness a signal was given, the projector stopped, the lights went on. The room waited in utter silence. Stahr's face was expressionless.

"Who wrote the scene?" he asked after a minute.

"Wylie White."

"Is he sober?"

"Sure he is."

Stahr considered.

"Put about four writers on that scene tonight," he said. "See who we've got. Is Sidney Howard here yet?"

"He got in this morning."

"Talk to him about it. Explain to him what I want there. The girl is in deadly terror—she's stalling. It's as simple as that. People don't have three emotions at once. And Kapper—"

The art director leaned his head forward out of the second row.

"Yeah."

"There's something the matter with that set."

There were little glances exchanged all over the room.

"What is it, Monroe?"

"You tell *me*," said Stahr. "It's crowded. It doesn't carry your eye out. It looks cheap."

"It wasn't."

"I know it wasn't. There's not much the matter but there's something. Go over and take a look tonight. It may be too much furniture—or the wrong kind. Perhaps a window would help. Couldn't you force the perspective in that hall a little more?"

"I'll see what I can do." Kapper edged his way out of the row looking at his watch.

"I'll have to get at it right away," he said. "I'll work tonight and we'll put it up in the morning."

"All right. Mort, you can shoot around those scenes, can't you?"

"I think so, Monroe."

"I take the blame for this. Have you got the fight stuff?"

"Coming up now."

Stahr nodded. Kapper hurried out and the room went dark again. On the screen four men staged a terrific socking match in a cellar. Stahr laughed.

"Look at Tracy," he said. "Look at him go down after that guy. I bet he's been in a few."

The men fought over and over. Always the same fight. Always at the end they faced each other smiling, sometimes touching the opponent in a friendly gesture on the shoulder. The only one in danger was the stunt man, a pug who could have murdered the other three. He was in danger only if they swung wild and didn't follow the blows he had taught them. Even so the youngest actor was afraid for his face and the director had covered his flinches with ingenious angles and interpositions.

And then two men met endlessly in a door, recognized each other and went on. They met, they started, they went on. They did it wrong. Again they met, they started, they went on.

Then a little girl read underneath a tree with a boy reading on a limb of the tree above. The little girl was bored and wanted to talk to the boy. He would pay no attention. The core of the apple he was eating fell on the little girl's head.

A voice spoke up out of the darkness:

"It's pretty long, isn't it, Monroe?"

"Not a bit," said Stahr. "It's nice. It has nice feeling."

"I just thought it was long."

"Sometimes ten feet can be too long—sometimes a scene two hundred feet long can be too short. I want to speak to the cutter before he touches this scene—this is something that'll be remembered in the picture."

The oracle had spoken. There was nothing to question or argue. Stahr must be right always, not most of the time, but always—or the structure would melt down like gradual butter.

Another hour passed. Dreams hung in fragments at the far end of the room, suffered analysis, passed—to be dreamed in crowds, or else discarded. The end was signalled by two tests, a character man and a girl. After the rushes, which had a tense rhythm of their own, the tests were smooth and finished—the observers settled in their chairs—Stahr's foot slipped to the floor. Opinions were welcome. One of the technical men let it be known that he would willingly cohabit with the girl—the rest were indifferent.

"Somebody sent up a test of that girl two years ago. She must be getting around—but she isn't getting any better. But the man's good. Can't we use him as the old Russian Prince in 'Steppes'?"

"He *is* an old Russian Prince," said the casting director. "But he's ashamed of it. He's a Red. And that's one part he says he wouldn't play."

"It's the only part he could play," said Stahr.

The lights went on. Stahr rolled his gum into its wrapper and put it in an ash-tray. He turned questioningly to his secretary.

"The processes on Stage 2," she said.

He looked in briefly at the processes, moving pictures taken against a background of other moving pictures by an ingenious device. There was a meeting in Marcus' office on the subject of "Manon" with a happy ending and Stahr had his say on that as he had before—it had been making money without a happy ending for a century and a half. He was obdurate—at this time in the afternoon he was at his most fluent and the opposition faded into another subject—they would lend a dozen stars to the benefit for those the quake had made homeless at Long Beach. In a sudden burst of giving five of them all at once made up a purse of twenty-five thousand dollars. They gave well but not as poor men give. It was not charity.

At his office there was word from the oculist to whom he had sent Pete Zavras that the camera man's eyes were 20/19, approximately perfect. He had written a letter that Zavras was having photostated. Stahr walked around his office cockily while Miss Doolan admired him. Prince Agge had dropped in to thank him for his afternoon on the sets and while they talked a cryptic word came from a supervisor that some writers named Marquand had "found out" and were about to quit.

"These are good writers," Stahr explained to Prince Agge. "And we don't have good writers out here."

"Why you can hire anyone!" exclaimed his visitor in surprise.

"Oh we hire them but when they get out here they're not good writers—so we have to work with the material we have."

"Like what?"

"Anybody that'll accept the system and stay decently sober—we have all sorts of people—disappointed poets, one-hit playwrights, college girls—we put them on an idea in pairs and if it slows down we put two more writers working behind them. I've had as many as three pairs working independently on the same idea."

"Do they like that?"

"Not if they know about it. They're not geniuses—none of them could make as much any other way. But these Marquands are a husband and wife team from the East—pretty good playwrights. They've just found out they're not alone on the story and it shocks them—shocks their sense of unity—that's the word they'll use."

"But what does make the—the unity?"

Stahr hesitated—his face was grim except that his eyes twinkled.

"I'm the unity," he said. "Come and see us again."

He saw the Marquands. He told them he liked their work, looking at Mrs. Marquand as if he could read her handwriting through the typescript. He told them kindly that he was taking them from the picture and putting them on another where there was less pressure, more time. As he had half expected they begged to stay on the first picture, seeing a quicker credit even though it was shared with others. The system was a shame, he admitted—gross, commercial, to be deplored. He had originated it—a fact that he did not mention.

When they had gone Miss Doolan came in triumphant.

"Mr. Stahr, the lady with the belt is on the phone."

Stahr walked in to his office alone and sat down behind his desk and picked up the phone with a great sinking of his stomach. He did not know what he wanted. He had not thought about the matter as he had thought of the matter of Pete Zavras. At first he had only wanted to know if they were "professional" people, if the woman was an actress who had got herself up to look like Minna as he had once had a young actress made up like Claudette Colbert and photographed her from the same angles.

"Hello," he said.

"Hello."

As he searched the short, rather surprised word for a vibration of last night, the feeling of terror began to steal over him and he choked it off with an effort of will.

"Well—you were hard to find," he said. "*Smith*—and you moved here recently. That was all we had. And a silver belt."

"Oh yes," the voice said, still uneasy, unpoised, "I had on a silver belt last night."

Now, where from here?

"Who *are* you?" the voice said, with a touch of flurried bourgeois dignity.

"My name is Monroe Stahr," he said.

A pause. It was a name that never appeared on the screen and she seemed to have trouble placing it.

"Oh yes—yes. You were the husband of Minna Davis."

"Yes."

Was it a trick? As the whole vision of last night came back to him—the very skin with that peculiar radiance as if phosphorus had touched it, he thought if it were a trick to reach him from somewhere. Not Minna and yet Minna. The curtains blew suddenly into the room, the papers whispered on his desk and his heart cringed faintly at the intense reality of the day outside his window. If he could go out now this way what would happen if he saw her again—the starry veiled expression, the mouth strongly formed for poor brave human laughter.

"I'd like to see you. Would you like to come to the studio?"

Again the hesitancy—then a blank refusal.

"Oh, I don't think I ought to. I'm awfully sorry."

This last was purely formal, a brush off, a final axe. Ordinary skin-deep vanity came to Stahr's aid, adding persuasion to his urgency.

"I'd like to see you," he said. "There's a reason."

"Well—I'm afraid that—"

"Could I come and see you?"

A pause again not from hesitation, he felt, but to assemble her answer.

"There's something you don't know," she said finally.

"Oh, you're probably married." He was impatient. "It has nothing to do with that. I asked you to come here openly, bring your husband if you have one."

"It's—it's quite impossible."

"Why?"

"I feel silly even talking to you but your secretary insisted—I thought I'd dropped something in the flood last night and you'd found it."

"I want very much to see you for five minutes."

"To put me in the movies."

"That wasn't my idea."

There was such a long pause that he thought he had offended her.

"Where could I meet you?" she asked unexpectedly.

"Here? At your house?"

"No—somewhere outside."

Suddenly Stahr could think of no place. His own house—a restaurant. Where did people meet—a house of assignation, a cocktail bar?

"I'll meet you somewhere at nine o'clock," she said.

"That's impossible, I'm afraid."

"Then never mind."

"All right then nine o'clock, but can we make it near here? There's a drug store on Wilshire—"

It was quarter to six. There were two men outside who had come every day at this time only to be postponed. This was an hour of fatigue—the men's business was not so important that it must be seen to, nor so insignificant that it could be ignored. So he postponed it again and sat motionless at his desk for a moment thinking about Russia. Not so much about Russia as about the picture about Russia which would consume a hopeless half hour presently. He knew there were many stories about Russia, not to mention The Story, and he had employed a squad of writers and research men for over a year but all the stories involved had the wrong feel. He felt it could be told in terms of the American thirteen states but it kept coming out different, in new terms that opened unpleasant possibilities and problems. He considered he was very fair to Russia—he had no desire to make anything but a sympathetic picture but it kept turning into a headache.

"Mr. Stahr—Mr. Drummon's outside and Mr. Kirstoff and Mrs. Cornhill about the Russian picture."

"All right—send them in."

Afterwards from six-thirty to seven-thirty he watched the afternoon rushes. Except for his engagement with the girl he would ordinarily have spent the early evening in the projection room or the dubbing room but it had been a late night with the earthquake and he decided to go to dinner. Coming in through his front office he found Pete Zavras waiting, his arm in a sling.

"You are the Aeschylus and the Diogenes of the moving picture," said Zavras simply. "Also the Asclepius and the Menander."

He bowed.

"Who are they?" asked Stahr smiling.

"They are my countrymen."

"I didn't know you made pictures in Greece."

"You're joking with me, Monroe," said Zavras. "I want to say you are as dandy a fellow as they come. You have saved me one hundred percent."

"You feel all right now?"

"My arm is nothing. It feels like someone kisses me there. It was worth doing what I did if this is the outcome."

"How did you happen to do it here?" Stahr asked curiously.

"Before the oracle," said Zavras. "The solver of Eleusinian mysteries. I wish I had my hands on the son-of-a-bitch who started the story."

"You make me sorry I didn't get an education," said Stahr.

"It isn't worth a damn," said Pete. "I took my baccalaureate in Salonika and look how I ended up."

"Not quite," said Stahr.

"If you want anybody's throat cut anytime day or night," said Zavras, "my number is in the book."

Stahr closed his eyes and opened them again. Zavras' silhouette had blurred a little against the sun. He hung on to the table behind him and said in an ordinary voice:

"Good luck, Pete."

The room was almost black but he made his feet move following a pattern into his office and waited till the door clicked shut before he felt for the pills. The water decanter clattered against the table; the glass clacked. He sat down in a big chair waiting for the benzedrine to take effect before he went to dinner.

Episode 12

As Stahr walked back from the commissary a hand waved at him from an open roadster. From the heads showing over the back he recognized a young actor and his girl, and watched them disappear through the gate already part of the summer twilight. Little by little he was losing the feel of such things, until it seemed that Minna had taken their poignancy with her; his apprehension of splendor was fading so that presently the luxury of eternal mourning would depart. A childish association of Minna with the material heavens made him, when he reached his office, order out his roadster for the first time this year. The big limousine seemed heavy with remembered conferences or exhausted sleep.

Leaving the studio he was still tense but the open car pulled the summer evening up close and he looked at it. There was a moon down at the end of the boulevard and it was a good illusion that it was a different moon every evening, every year. Other lights shone in Hollywood since Minna's death: in the open markets lemons and grapefruit and green apples slanted a misty glare into the street. Ahead of him the stop-signal of a car winked violet and at another crossing he watched it wink again. Everywhere floodlights raked the sky. On an empty corner two mysterious men moved a gleaming drum in pointless arcs over the heavens.

In the drug store a woman stood by the candy counter. She was tall, almost as tall as Stahr, and embarrassed. Obviously it was a situation for her and if Stahr had not looked as he did—most considerate and polite—she would not have gone through with it. They said hello and walked out without another word, scarcely a glance— yet before they reached the curb Stahr knew: this was just exactly a pretty American woman and nothing more—no beauty like Minna.

"Where are we going?" she asked. "I thought there'd be a chauffeur. Never mind—I'm a good boxer."

"Boxer?"

"That didn't sound very polite." She forced a smile. "But you people are supposed to be such *horrors*."

The conception of himself as sinister amused Stahr—then suddenly it failed to amuse him.

"Why did you want to see me?" she asked as she got in.

He stood motionless, wanting to tell her get out immediately. But she had relaxed in the car and he knew the unfortunate situation was of his own making—he shut his teeth and walked around to get in. The street lamp fell full upon her face and it was difficult to believe that this was the girl of last night. He saw no resemblance to Minna at all.

"I'll run you home," he said. "Where do you live?"

"Run me home?" She was startled. "There's no hurry—I'm sorry if I offended you."

"No. It was nice of you to come. I've been stupid. Last night I had an idea that you were an exact double for someone I knew. It was dark and the light was in my eyes."

She was offended—he had reproached her for not looking like someone else.

"It was just that!" she said. "That's funny."

They rode in silence for a minute.

"You were married to Minna Davis, weren't you?" she said with a flash of intuition. "Excuse me for referring to it."

He was driving as fast as he could without making it conspicuous.

"I'm quite a different type from Minna Davis," she said, "—if that's who you meant. You might have referred to the girl who was with me. She looks more like Minna Davis than I do."

That was of no interest now. The thing was to get this over quick and forget it.

"Could it have been her?" she asked. "She lives next door."

"Not possibly," he said. "I remember the silver belt you wore."

"That was me all right."

They were northwest of Sunset, climbing one of the canyons

through the hills. Lighted bungalows rose along the winding road and the electric current that animated them sweated into the evening air as radio sound.

"You see that last highest light—Kathleen lives there. I live just over the top of the hill."

A moment later she said, "Stop here."

"I thought you said over the top."

"I want to stop at Kathleen's."

"I'm afraid I'm—"

"I want to get out here myself," she said impatiently.

Stahr slid out after her. She started toward a new little house almost roofed over by a single willow tree, and automatically he followed her to the steps. She rang a bell and turned to say good night.

"I'm sorry you were disappointed," she said.

He was sorry for her now—sorry for them both.

"It was my fault. Good night."

A wedge of light came out the opening door and as a girl's voice inquired "Who is it?" Stahr looked up.

There she was—face and form and smile against the light from inside. It was Minna's face—the skin with its peculiar radiance as if phosphorus had touched it, the mouth with its warm line that never counted costs—and over all the haunting jollity that had fascinated a generation.

With a leap his heart went out of him as it had the night before, only this time it stayed out there with a vast beneficence.

"Oh Edna you can't come in," the girl said. "I've been cleaning and the house is full of ammonia smell."

Edna began to laugh, bold and loud. "I believe it was you he wanted to see, Kathleen," she said.

Stahr's eyes and Kathleen's met and tangled. For an instant they made love as no one ever dares to do after. Their glance was closer than an embrace, more urgent than a call.

"He telephoned me," said Edna. "It seems he thought—" Stahr interrupted, stepping forward into the light.

"I was afraid we were rude at the studio, yesterday evening."

But there were no words for what he really said. She listened closely without shame. Life flared high in them both—Edna seemed at a distance and in darkness.

"You weren't rude," said Kathleen. A cool wind blew the brown curls around her forehead. "We had no business there."

"I hope you'll both—," Stahr said, "—come and make a tour of the studio."

"Who are you? Somebody important?"

"He was Minna Davis' husband, he's a producer," said Edna as if it were a rare joke, "—and this isn't at all what he just told me. I think he has a crush on you."

"Shut up, Edna," said Kathleen sharply.

As if suddenly realizing her offensiveness Edna said "Phone me, will you?" and stalked away toward the road. But she carried their secret with her—she had seen a spark pass between them in the darkness.

"I remember you," Kathleen said to Stahr. "You got us out of the flood."

—Now what? The other woman was more missed in her absence. They were alone and on too slim a basis for what had passed already. They existed nowhere. His world seemed far away—she had no world at all except the idol's head, the half open door.

"You're Irish," he said, trying to build one for her.

She nodded.

"I've lived in London a long time—I didn't think you could tell."

The wild green eyes of a bus sped up the road in the darkness. They were silent until it went by.

"Your friend Edna didn't like me," he said. "I think it was the word Producer."

"She's just come out here too. She's a silly creature who means no harm. *I* shouldn't be afraid of you."

She searched his face. She thought, like everyone, that he seemed tired—then she forgot it at the impression he gave of a brazier out of doors on a cool night.

"I suppose the girls are all after you to put them on the screen."

"They've given up," he said.

This was an understatement—they were all there, he knew, just over his threshold, but they had been there so long that their clamoring voices were no more than the sound of the traffic in the street. But his position remained more than royal—a king could make only one queen—Stahr, at least so they supposed, could make many.

"I'm thinking that it would turn you into a cynic," she said. "You didn't want to put me in the pictures."

"No."

"That's good. I'm no actress. Once in London a man came up to me in the Carlton and asked me to make a test but I thought awhile and finally I didn't go."

They had been standing nearly motionless, as if in a moment he would leave and she would go in. Stahr laughed suddenly.

"I feel as if I had my foot in the door—like a collector."

She laughed too.

"I'm sorry I can't ask you in. Shall I get my reefer and sit outside?"

"No." He scarcely knew why he felt it was time to go. He might see her again—he might not. It was just as well this way.

"You'll come to the studio?" he said. "I can't promise to go around with you, but if you come you must be sure to send word to my office."

A frown, the shadow of a hair in breadth, appeared between her eyes.

"I'm not sure," she said. "But I'm very much obliged."

He knew that, for some reason, she would not come—in an instant she had slipped away from him. They both sensed that the moment was played out. He must go, even though he went nowhere and left with nothing. Practically, vulgarly, he did not have her telephone number—or even her name, but it seemed impossible to ask for them now.

She walked with him to the car, her glowing beauty and her unexplored novelty pressing up against him, but there was a foot of moonlight between them when they came out of the shadow.

"Is this all?" he said spontaneously.

He saw regret in her face—but there was a flick of the lip also, a bending of the smile toward some indirection, a momentary dropping and lifting of a curtain over a forbidden passage.

"I do hope we'll meet again," she said almost formally.

"I'd be sorry if we didn't."

They were distant for a moment. But as he turned his car in the next drive and came back with her still waiting, and waved and drove on he felt exalted and happy. He was glad that there was beauty in the world that would not be weighed in the scales of the casting department.

But at home he felt a curious loneliness as his butler made him tea in the samovar. It was the old hurt come back, heavy and delightful. When he took up the first of two scripts that were his evening stint, that presently he would visualize line by line on the screen, he waited a moment, thinking of Minna. He explained to her that it was really nothing, that no one could ever be like she was, that he was sorry.

That was substantially a day of Stahr's. I don't know about the illness, when it started, etc., because he was secretive but I know he fainted a couple of times that month because Father told me. Prince Agge is my authority for the luncheon in the commissary where he told them he was going to make a picture that would lose money— which was something considering the men he had to deal with and that he held a big block of stock and had a profit sharing contract.

And Wylie White told me a lot which I believed because he felt Stahr intensely with a mixture of jealousy and admiration. As for me I was head over heels in love with him then and you can take what I say for what it's worth.

Episode 13

Fresh as the morning I went up to see him a week later. Or so I thought; when Wylie called for me I had gotten into riding clothes to give the impression I'd been out in the dew since early morning.

"I'm going to throw myself under the wheel of Stahr's car, this morning," I said.

"How about this car," he suggested. "It's one of the best cars Mort Flieshacker ever sold second hand."

"Not on your flowing veil," I answered like a book. "You have a wife in the East."

"She's the past," he said. "You've got one great card, Celia—your valuation of yourself. Do you think anybody would look at you if you weren't Pat Brady's daughter?"

We don't take abuse like our mothers would have. Nothing—no remark from a contemporary means much. They tell you to be smart they're marrying you for your money or you tell them. Everything's simpler. Or is it? as we used to say.

But as I turned on the radio and the car raced up Laurel Canyon to "The Thundering Beat of My Heart," I didn't believe he was right. I had good features except my face was too round and a skin they seemed to love to touch and good legs and I didn't have to wear a brassiere. I haven't a sweet nature but who was Wylie to reproach me for that.

"Don't you think I'm smart to go in the morning?" I asked.

"Yeah. To the busiest man in California. He'll appreciate it. Why didn't you wake him up at four?"

"That's just it. At night he's tired. He's been looking at people all day and some of them not bad. I come in in the morning and start a train of thought."

"I don't like it. It's brazen."

"What have you got to offer? And don't be rough."

"I love you," he said without much conviction. "I love you more than I love your money and that's plenty. Maybe your father would make me a supervisor."

"I could marry the last man tapped for Bones this year and live in Southampton."

I turned the dial and got either "Gone" or "Lost"—there were good songs that year. The music was getting better again. When I was young during the Depression it wasn't so hot and the best numbers were from the twenties like Benny Goodman playing "Blue Heaven" or Paul Whiteman with "When Day Is Done." There were only the bands to listen to. But now I liked almost everything except Father singing "Little Girl, You've Had a Busy Day" to try to create a sentimental father-and-daughter feeling.

"Lost" and "Gone" were the wrong mood so I turned again and

got "Lovely To Look At" which was my kind of poetry. I looked back as we crossed the crest of the foothills—with the air so clear you could see the leaves on Sunset Mountain two miles away. It's startling to you sometimes—just air, unobstructed, uncomplicated air.

"Lovely to look at—de—lightful to know-w-w," I sang.

"Are you going to sing for Stahr?" Wylie said. "If you do, get in a line about my being a good supervisor."

"Oh, this'll be only Stahr and me," I said. "He's going to look at me and think 'I've never really seen her before.' "

"We don't use that line this year," he said.

"—Then he'll say 'Little Celia' like he did the night of the earthquake. He'll say he never noticed I have become a woman."

"You won't have to do a thing."

"I'll stand there and bloom. After he kisses me as you would a child—"

"That's all in my script," complained Wylie. "And I've got to show it to him tomorrow."

"—he'll sit down and put his face in his hands and say he never thought of me like that."

"You mean you get in a little fast work during the kiss."

"I bloom, I told you. How often do I have to tell you I bloom."

"It's beginning to sound pretty randy to me," said Wylie. "How about laying off—I've got to work this morning."

"Then he says it seems as if he was always meant to be this way."

"Right in the industry. Producer's blood." He pretended to shiver. "I'd hate to have a transfusion of that."

"Then he says—"

"I know all his lines," said Wylie. "What I want to know is what you say."

"Somebody comes in," I went on.

"And you jump up quickly off the casting couch smoothing your skirts."

"Do you want me to walk out and get home?"

We were in Beverly Hills, getting very beautiful now with the tall Hawaiian pines. Hollywood is a perfectly zoned city so you know exactly what kind of people economically live in each section from executives and directors, through technicians in their bungalows right down to extras. This was the executive section and a very fancy lot of pastry. It wasn't as romantic as the dingiest village of Virginia or New Hampshire but it looked nice this morning.

"They asked me how I knew," sang the radio, "—my true love was true."

My heart was fire and smoke was in my eyes and everything but I figured my chance at about fifty-fifty. I would walk right up to him as if I was either going to walk through him or kiss him in the mouth—and stop a bare foot away and say Hello with disarming understatement.

And I did—though of course it wasn't like I expected. Stahr's beautiful dark eyes looking back into mine, knowing I am dead sure everything I was thinking—and not a bit embarrassed. I stood there an hour, I think, without moving and all he did was twitch the side of his mouth and put his hands in his pockets.

"Will you go with me to the ball tonight?" I asked.

"What ball?"

"The screen-writers' ball down at the Ambassador."

"Oh yes." He considered. "I can't go with you. I might just come in late. We've got a sneak preview in Glendale."

How different it all was than what you've planned. When he sat down I went over and put my head among his telephones like a sort of desk appendage and looked at him and his dark eyes looked back so kind and nothing. Men don't often know those times when a girl could be had for nothing. All I succeeded in putting into his head was:

"Why don't you get married, Celia?"

Maybe he'd bring up Robby again, try to make a match there.

"What could I do to interest an interesting man?" I asked him.

"Tell him you're in love with him."

"Should I chase him?"

"Yes," he said smiling.

"I don't know. If it isn't there it isn't there."

"I'd marry you," he said unexpectedly. "I'm lonesome as hell. But I'm too old and tired to undertake anything."

I went around the desk and stood beside him.

"Undertake me."

He looked up in surprise, understanding for the first time that I was in deadly earnest.

"Oh no," he said. He looked almost miserable for a minute. "Pictures are my girl. I haven't got much time—" He corrected himself quickly, "I mean any time. It'd be like marrying a doctor."

"You couldn't love me."

"It's not that," he said and—right out of my dream but with a difference, "I never thought of you that way, Celia. I've known you so long. Somebody told me you were going to marry Wylie White."

"And you had—no reaction."

"Yes, I did. I was going to speak to you about it. Wait till he's been sober for two years."

"I'm not even considering it, Monroe."

We were way off the track, and just as in my day-dream somebody came in—only I was quite sure Stahr had pressed a concealed button.

I'll always think of that moment, when I felt Miss Doolan behind me with her pad, as the end of childhood, the end of the time when you cut out pictures. What I was looking at wasn't Stahr but a picture of him I cut out over and over: the eyes that flashed a sophisticated understanding at you and then darted up too soon into his wide brow with its ten thousand plots and plans; the face that was ageing from within, so that there were no casual furrows of worry and vexation but a drawn asceticism as if from a silent self-set struggle—or a long illness. It was handsomer to me than all the rosy tan from Coronado to Del Monte. He was my picture, as sure as if he was pasted on the inside of my old locker in school. That's what I told Wylie White and when a girl tells the man she likes second best about the other one—then she's in love.

13 (continued)

I noticed the girl long before Stahr arrived at the dance. Not a pretty girl, for there are none of those in Los Angeles—one girl can be pretty but a dozen are only a chorus. Nor yet a professional beauty—they do all the breathing for everyone and finally even the men have to go outside for air. Just a girl, with the skin of one of Raphael's corner angels and a style that made you look back twice to see if it were something she had on.

I noticed her and forgot her. She was sitting back behind the pillars at a table whose ornament was a faded semi-star who, in hopes of being noticed and getting a bit, rose and danced regularly with some scarecrow males. It reminded me shamefully of my first party where Mother made me dance over and over with the same boy to keep in the spotlight. The semi-star spoke to several people at our table but we were busy being Cafe Society and she got nowhere at all.

From our angle it appeared that they all wanted something.

"You're expected to fling it around," said Wylie, "—like in the old days. When they find out you're hanging on to it they get discouraged. That's what all this brave gloom is about—the only way to keep their self respect is to be Hemingway characters. But underneath they hate you in a mournful way and you know it."

He was right—I knew that since 1933 the rich could only be happy alone together.

I saw Stahr come into the half-light at the top of the wide steps and stand there with his hands in his pockets looking around. It was late and the lights seemed to have burned a little lower, though they were the same. The floor show was finished except for a man who still wore a placard which said that at midnight in the Hollywood Bowl Sonja Henie was going to skate on hot soup. You could see the sign as he danced becoming less and less funny on his back. A few years before there would have been drunks around. The faded actress seemed to be looking for them hopefully over her partner's shoulder. I followed her with my eyes when she went back to her table—

—and there, to my surprise, was Stahr talking to the other girl. They were smiling at each other as if this was the beginning of the world.

Stahr had expected nothing like this when he stood at the head of the steps a few minutes earlier. The sneak preview had disappointed him and afterwards he had had a scene with Jaques La Borwits right in front of the theatre for which he was now sorry. He had started toward the Brady party when he saw Kathleen sitting in the middle of a long white table alone.

Immediately things changed. As he walked toward her the people shrank back against the walls till they were only murals; the white table lengthened and became an altar where the priestess sat alone. Vitality welled up in him and he could have stood a long time across the table from her, looking and smiling.

The incumbents of the table were crawling back—Stahr and Kathleen danced.

When she came close his several visions of her blurred; she was momentarily unreal. Usually a girl's skull made her real but not this time—Stahr continued to be dazzled as they danced out along the floor—to the last edge, where they stepped through a mirror into another dance with new dancers whose faces were familiar but nothing more. In this new region he talked, fast and urgently.

"What's your name?"

"Kathleen Moore."

"Kathleen Moore," he repeated.

"I have no telephone, if that's what you're thinking."

"When will you come to the studio?"

"It's not possible. Truly."

"Why isn't it? Are you married?"

"No."

"You're not married?"

"No, nor never have been. But then I may be."

"Someone there at the table."

"No." She laughed. "What curiosity!"

But she was deep in it with him, no matter what the words were. Her eyes invited him to a romantic communion of unbelievable intensity. As if she realized this she said, frightened:

"I must go back now. I promised this dance."

"I don't want to lose you. Couldn't we have lunch or dinner?"

"It's impossible." But her expression helplessly amended the words to "It's just possible. The door is still open by a chink if you could squeeze past. But quickly—so little time."

"I must go back," she repeated aloud. Then she dropped her arms, stopped dancing and looked at him, a laughing wanton.

"When I'm with you I don't breathe quite right," she said.

She turned, picked up her long dress, and stepped back through the mirror. Stahr followed until she stopped near her table.

"Thank you for the dance," she said. "And now really, good night."

Then she nearly ran.

Stahr went to the table where he was expected and sat down with the Cafe Society group—from Wall Street, Grand Street, Loudoun County Virginia, and Odessa Russia. They were all talking with enthusiasm about a horse that had run very fast and Mr. Marcus was the most enthusiastic of all. Stahr guessed that Jews had taken over the worship of horses as a super-symbol—for years it had been the Cossacks mounted and the Jews on foot. Now the Jews had horses and it gave them a sense of extraordinary well-being and power. Stahr sat pretending to listen and even nodding when something was referred to him, but all the time watching the table behind the pillars. If everything had not happened as it had, even to his connecting the silver belt with the wrong girl, he might have thought it was some elaborate frame-up. But the elusiveness was beyond suspicion. For there in a moment he saw that she was escaping again—the pantomime at the table indicated good bye. She was leaving, she was gone.

"There—" said Wylie White with malice, "—goes Cinderella. Simply bring the slipper to the Regal Shoe Co., 812 South Broadway."

Stahr overtook her in the long upper lobby where middle-aged women sat behind a roped-off space, watching the ballroom entrance.

"Am I responsible for this?" he asked.

"I was going anyhow." But she added almost resentfully, "They talked as if I'd been dancing with the Prince of Wales. They all stared at me. One of the men wanted to draw my picture and another one wanted to see me tomorrow."

"That's just what I want," said Stahr gently. "But I want to see you much more than he does."

"You insist so," she said wearily. "One reason I left England was that men always wanted their own way. I thought it was different here. Isn't it enough that I don't want to see you?"

"Ordinarily," agreed Stahr. "Please believe me, I'm way out of my depth already. I feel like a fool. But I must see you again and talk to you."

She hesitated.

"There's no reason for feeling like a fool," she said. "You're too good a man to feel like a fool. But you should see this for what it is."

"What is it?"

"You've fallen for me—completely. You've got me in your dreams."

"I'd forgotten you," he declared, "—till the moment I walked in that door."

"Forgotten me with your head perhaps. But I knew the first time I saw you that you were the kind that likes me—"

She stopped herself. Near them a man and woman from the party were saying good bye: "Tell her hello—tell her I love her dearly," said the woman, "you both—all of you—the children." Stahr could not talk like that, the way everyone talked now. He could think of nothing further to say as they walked toward the elevator except:

"I suppose you're perfectly right."

"Oh, you admit it?"

"No, I don't," he retracted. "It's just the whole way you're made. What you say—how you walk—the way you look right this minute—" He saw she had melted a little and his hopes rose. "To-morrow is Sunday and usually I work on Sunday but if there's anything you're curious about in Hollywood, any person you want to meet or see, please let me arrange it."

They were standing by the elevator. It opened but she let it go.

"You're very modest," she said. "You always talk about showing me the studio and taking me around. Don't you ever stay alone?"

"Tomorrow I'll feel very much alone."

"Oh, the poor man—I could weep for him. He could have all the stars jumping around him and he chooses me."

He smiled—he had laid himself open to that one.

The elevator came again. She signalled for it to wait.

"I'm a weak woman," she said. "If I meet you tomorrow will you leave me in peace? No, you won't. You'll make it worse. It wouldn't do any good but harm so I'll say no and thank you."

She got into the elevator. Stahr got in too and they smiled as they dropped two floors to the hall cross-sectioned with small shops. Down at the end, held back by police was the crowd, their heads and shoulders leaning forward to look down the alley. Kathleen shivered.

"They looked so strange when I came in," she said, "—as if they were furious at me for not being someone famous."

"I know another way out," said Stahr.

They went through a drug store, down an alley and came out into the clear cool California night beside the car park. He felt detached from the dance now and she did too.

"A lot of picture people used to live down here," he said. "John Barrymore and Pola Negri in those bungalows. And Connie Talmadge lived in that tall thin apartment house over the way."

"Doesn't anybody live here now?"

"The studios moved out into the country," he said. "What used to be the country. I had some good times around here though."

He did not mention that ten years ago Minna and her mother had lived in another apartment over the way.

"How old are you?" she asked suddenly.

"I've lost track—almost thirty-five I think."

"They said at the table you were the boy wonder."

"I'll be that when I'm sixty," he said grimly. "You will meet me tomorrow, won't you?"

"I'll meet you," she said. "Where?"

Suddenly there was no place to meet. She would not go to a party at anyone's house, nor to the country, nor swimming though she hesitated, nor to a well-known restaurant. She seemed hard to please but he knew there was some reason. He would find out in time. It occurred to him that she might be the sister or daughter of someone well-known, who was pledged to keep in the background. He suggested that he come for her and they could decide.

"That wouldn't do," she said. "What about right here—the same spot."

He nodded—pointing up at the arch under which they stood.

He put her into her car which would have brought eighty dollars from any kindly dealer, and watched it rasp away. Down by the entrance a cheer went up as a favorite emerged, and Stahr wondered whether to show himself and say good night.

This is Cecelia taking up the narrative in person. Stahr came back finally—it was about half past three—and asked me to dance.

"How are you?" he asked me, just as if he hadn't seen me that morning. "I got involved in a long conversation with a man."

It was secret too—he cared that much about it.

"I took him to ride," he went on innocently. "I didn't realize how much this part of Hollywood had changed."

"Has it changed?"

"Oh yes," he said. "Changed completely. Unrecognizable. I couldn't tell you exactly but it's all changed—everything. It's like a new city." After a moment he amplified, "I had no idea how much it had changed."

"Who was the man?" I ventured.

"An old friend," he said vaguely. "Someone I knew a long time ago."

I had made Wylie try to find out quietly who she was. He had gone over and the ex-star had asked him excitedly to sit down. No—she didn't know who the girl was—a friend of a friend of someone—even the man who had brought her didn't know.

So Stahr and I danced to the beautiful music of Glenn Miller playing "I'm on a See-saw." It was good dancing now with plenty of room. But it was lonely—lonelier than before the girl had gone. For me, as well as for Stahr, she took the evening with her, took along the stabbing pain I had felt—left the great ball-room empty and without emotion. Now it was nothing and I was dancing with an absent minded man who told me how much Los Angeles had changed.

Section 14

They met, next afternoon, as strangers in an unfamiliar country. Last night was gone, the girl he had danced with was gone. A misty rose-and-blue hat with a trifling veil came along the terrace to him and paused, searching his face. Stahr was strange too in a brown suit and black tie that blocked him out more tangibly than a formal dinner coat, or when he was simply a face and voice in the darkness when they first met.

He was the first to be sure it was the same person as before—the upper half of the face that was Minna's, luminous, with creamy temples and opalescent brow—the coco-colored curly hair. He could have put his arm around her and pulled her close with an almost family familiarity—already he knew the down on her neck, the very set of her backbone, the corners of her eyes and how she breathed—the very texture of the clothes that she would wear.

"Did you wait here all night?" she said, in a voice that was like a whisper.

"I didn't move—didn't stir."

Still a problem remained, the same one—there was no special place to go.

"I'd like tea," she suggested, "—if it's some place you're not known."

"That sounds as if one of us had a bad reputation."

"Doesn't it?" she laughed.

"We'll go to the shore," Stahr suggested. "There's a place there where I got out once and was chased by a trained seal."

"Do you think the seal could make tea?"

"Well—he's trained. And I don't think he'll talk—I don't think his training got that far. What in *hell* are you trying to hide?"

After a moment she said lightly, "Perhaps the future," in a way that might mean anything or nothing at all.

As they drove away she pointed at her jalopy in the parking lot.

"Do you think it's safe?"

"I doubt it. I noticed some black-bearded foreigners snooping around."

Kathleen looked at him alarmed.

"Really?" She saw he was smiling. "I believe everything you say," she said. "You've got such a gentle way about you that I don't see why they're all so afraid of you." She examined him with approval—fretting a little about his pallor, which was accentuated by the bright afternoon. "Do you work very hard? Do you really always work on Sundays?"

He responded to her interest—impersonal yet not perfunctory.

"Not always. Once we had—we had a house with a pool and all—and people came on Sunday. I played tennis and swam. I don't swim any more."

"Why not? It's good for you. I thought all Americans swam."

"My legs got very thin—a few years ago and it embarrassed me. There were other things I used to do—lots of things. I used to play handball when I was a kid, and sometimes out here—I had a court that was washed away in a storm."

"You have a good build," she said in formal compliment, meaning only that he was made with thin grace.

He rejected this with a shake of his head.

"I enjoy working most," he said. "My work is very congenial."

"Did you always want to be in movies?"

"No. When I was young I wanted to be a chief clerk—the one who knew where everything was."

She smiled.

"That's odd. And now you're much more than that."

"No, I'm still a chief clerk," Stahr said. "That's my gift, if I have one. Only when I got to be it I found out that no one knew where anything was. And I found out that you had to know why it was where it was, and whether it should be left there. They began throwing it all at me and it was a very complex office. Pretty soon I had all the keys. And they wouldn't have remembered what locks they fitted if I gave them back."

They stopped for a red light and a newsboy bleated at them: "Mickey Mouse Murdered! Randolph Hearst declares war on China!"

"We'll have to buy his paper," she said.

As they drove on she straightened her hat and preened herself. Seeing him looking at her she smiled.

She was alert and calm—qualities that were currently at a premium. There was lassitude in plenty—California was filling up with weary desperadoes. And there were tense young men and women who lived back East in spirit while they carried on a losing battle against the climate. But it was everyone's secret that sustained effort was difficult here—a secret that Stahr scarcely admitted to himself. But he knew that people from other places spurted a pure rill of new energy for a while.

They were very friendly now. She had not made a move or a gesture that was out of keeping with her beauty, that pressed it out of its contour one way or another. It was all proper to itself. He judged her as he would a shot in a picture. She was not trash, she was not confused but clear—in his special meaning of the word which implied balance, delicacy and proportion, she was "nice."

They reached Santa Monica where there were the stately houses of a dozen picture stars, penned in the middle of a crawling Coney Island. They turned down hill into the wide blue sky and sea and went on along the sea till the beach slid out again from under the bathers in a widening and narrowing yellow strand.

"I'm building a house out here," Stahr said. "Much further on. I don't know why I'm building it."

"Perhaps it's for me," she said.

"Maybe it is."

"I think it's splendid for you to build a big house for me without even knowing what I looked like."

"It isn't so big. And it hasn't any roof. I didn't know what kind of roof you wanted."

"We don't want a roof. They told me it never rained here. It—"

She stopped so suddenly that he knew she was reminded of something.

"Just something that's past," she said.

"What was it?" he demanded. "Another house without a roof?"

"Yes. Another house without a roof."

"Were you happy there?"

"I lived with a man," she said. "A long, long time—too long. It was one of those awful mistakes people make. I lived with him a long time after I wanted to get out but he couldn't let me go. He'd try but he couldn't. So finally I ran away."

He was listening, weighing but not judging. Nothing changed under the rose-and-blue hat. She was twenty-five or so. It would have been a waste if she had not loved and been loved.

"We were too close," she said. "We should probably have had children—to stand between us. But you can't have children when there's no roof to the house."

All right, he knew something of her. It would not be like last night when something kept saying, as in a story conference: "We know nothing about the girl. We don't have to know much—but we have to know something." A vague background spread behind her, something more tangible than the head of Siva in the moonlight.

They came to the restaurant, forbidding with many Sunday automobiles. When they got out the trained seal growled reminiscently at Stahr. The man who owned it said that the seal would never ride in the back seat of his car but always climbed over the back and up in front. It was plain that the man was in bondage to the seal, though he had not yet acknowledged it to himself.

"I'd like to see the house you're building," said Kathleen. "I don't want tea—tea is the past."

Kathleen drank a Coke instead and they drove on ten miles into a sun so bright that he took out two pairs of cheaters from a compartment. Five miles further on they turned down a small promontory and came to the fuselage of Stahr's house.

A headwind blowing out of the sun threw spray up the rocks and over the car. Concrete mixers, raw yellow wood and builders' rubble waited, an open wound in the sea-scape, for Sunday to be over. They walked around front where great boulders rose to what would be the terrace.

She looked at the feeble hills behind and winced faintly at the barren glitter, and Stahr saw—

"No use looking for what's not here," he said cheerfully. "Think of it as if you were standing on one of those globes with a map on it—I always wanted one when I was a boy."

"I understand," she said after a minute. "When you do that you can feel the earth turn, can't you."

He nodded.

"Yes. Otherwise it's all just mañana—waiting for the morning or the moon."

They went in under the scaffolding. One room, which was to be the chief salon, was completed even to the built-in book shelves and the curtain rods and the trap in the floor for the motion picture projection machine. And, to her surprise, this opened out to a porch with cushioned chairs in place and a ping-pong table. There was another ping-pong table on the newly laid turf beyond.

"Last week I gave a premature luncheon," he admitted. "I had some props brought out—some grass and things. I wanted to see how the place felt."

She laughed suddenly.

"Isn't that real grass?"

"Oh yes—it's grass."

Beyond the strip of anticipatory lawn was the excavation for a swimming pool, patronized now by a crowd of seagulls who saw them and took flight.

"Are you going to live here all alone?" she asked him. "Not even dancing girls?"

"Probably. I used to make plans but not any more. I thought this would be a nice place to read scripts. The studio is really home."

"That's what I've heard about American business men."

He caught a lilt of criticism in her voice.

"You do what you're born to do," he said gently. "About once a month somebody tries to reform me, tells me what a barren old age I'll have when I can't work any more. But it's not so simple."

The wind was rising. It was time to go and he had his car keys out of his pocket, absent mindedly jingling them in his hand. There was the silvery "Hey!" of a telephone, coming from somewhere across the sunshine.

It was not from the house and they hurried here and there around the garden like children playing warmer and colder—closing in finally on a tool shack by the tennis court. The phone, irked with delay, barked at them suspiciously from the wall. Stahr hesitated.

"Shall I let the damn thing ring?"

"I couldn't. Unless I was sure who it was."

"Either it's for somebody else or they've made a wild guess."

He picked up the receiver.

"Hello. . . . Long distance from where? Yes, this is Mr. Stahr."

His manner changed perceptibly. She saw what few people had seen for a decade—Stahr impressed. It was not discordant because he often pretended to be impressed but it made him momentarily a little younger.

"It's the President," he said to her, almost stiffly.

"Of your company?"

"No, of the United States."

He was trying to be casual for her benefit but his voice was eager.

"All right, I'll wait," he said into the phone, and then to Kathleen, "I've talked to him before."

She watched. He smiled at her and winked as an evidence that while he must give this his best attention he had not forgotten her.

"Hello," he said presently. He listened. Then he said "Hello" again. He frowned.

"Can you talk a little louder," he said politely, and then "Who? . . . What's that?"

She saw a disgusted look come into his face.

"I don't want to talk to him," he said. "No!"

He turned to Kathleen.

"Believe it or not, it's an orang-outang."

He waited while something was explained to him at length; then he repeated:

"I don't want to talk to it, Lew. I haven't got anything to say that would interest an orang-outang."

He beckoned to Kathleen and when she came close to the phone he held the receiver so that she heard odd breathing and a gruff growl. Then a voice:

"This is no phoney, Monroe. It can talk and it's a dead ringer for McKinley. Mr. Horace Wickersham is with me here with a picture of McKinley in his hand—"

Stahr listened patiently.

"We've got a chimp," he said after a minute. "He bit a chunk out of John Gilbert last year. . . . All right, put him on again."

He spoke formally as if to a child.

"Hello Orang-outang."

His face changed and he turned to Kathleen.

"He said hello."

"Ask him his name," suggested Kathleen.

"Hello Orang-outang—God, what a thing to be!—Do you know your name? . . . He doesn't seem to know his name. . . . Listen, Lew. We're not making anything like 'King Kong' and there is no monkey in 'The Hairy Ape.' . . . Of course I'm sure. I'm sorry, Lew, good bye."

He was annoyed with Lew because he had thought it was the President and changed his manner acting as if it were. He felt a little ridiculous but Kathleen felt sorry and liked him better because it had been an orang-outang.

SECTION 14 (2nd part)

They started back along the shore with the sun behind them. The house seemed kindlier when they left it, as if warmed by their visit—the hard glitter of the place was more endurable if they were not bound there like people on the shiny surface of a moon. Looking back from a curve of the shore, they saw the sky growing pink behind the indecisive structure and the point of land seemed a friendly island, not without promise of fine hours on a further day.

Past Malibu with its gaudy shacks and fishing barges they came into the range of human kind again, the cars stacked and piled along the road, the beaches like ant hills without a pattern, save for the dark drowned heads that sprinkled the sea.

Goods from the city were increasing in sight—blankets, matting, umbrellas, cookstoves, reticules full of clothing—the prisoners had laid out their shackles beside them on this sand. It was Stahr's sea if he wanted it, or knew what to do with it—only by sufferance did these others wet their feet and fingers in the wild cool reservoirs of man's world.

Stahr turned off the road by the sea and up a canyon and along a hill road and the people dropped away. The hill became the outskirts of the city. Stopping for gasoline he stood beside the car.

"We could have dinner," he said almost anxiously.

"You have work you could do."

"No—I haven't planned anything. Couldn't we have dinner?"

He knew that she had nothing to do either—no planned evening or special place to go.

She compromised.

"Do you want to get something in that drug store across the street?"

He looked at it tentatively.

"Is that really what you want?"

"I like to eat in American drug stores. It seems so queer and strange."

They sat on high stools and had tomato broth and hot sandwiches. It was more intimate than anything they had done and they both felt a dangerous sort of loneliness and felt it in each other. They shared in varied scents of the drug store, bitter and sweet and sour, and the mystery of the waitress with only the outer part of her hair dyed and black beneath, and when it was over, the still life of their empty plates—a sliver of potato, a sliced pickle and an olive stone.

It was dusk in the street, it seemed nothing to smile at him now when they got into the car.

"Thank you so much. It's been a nice afternoon."

It was not far from her house. They felt the beginning of the hill and the louder sound of the car in second was the beginning of the end. Lights were on in the climbing bungalows—he turned on the headlights of the car. Stahr felt heavy in the pit of his stomach.

"We'll go out again."

"No," she said quickly as if she had been expecting this. "I'll write you a letter. I'm sorry I've been so mysterious—it was really a compliment because I like you so much. You should try not to work so hard. You ought to marry again."

"Oh, that isn't what you should say," he broke out protestingly. "This has been you and me today. I may have meant nothing to you—it meant a lot to me. I'd like time to tell you about it."

But if he were to take time it must be in her house for they were there and she was shaking her head as the car drew up to the door.

"I must go now. I do have an engagement. I didn't tell you."

"That's not true. But it's all right."

He walked to the door with her and stood in his own footsteps of that other night while she felt in her bag for the key.

"Have you got it?"

"I've got it," she said.

That was the moment to go in but she wanted to see him once more and she leaned her head to the left, then to the right trying to catch his face against the last twilight. She leaned too far and too long and it was natural when his hand touched the back of her upper arm and shoulder and pressed her forward into the darkness of his throat. She shut her eyes feeling the bevel of the key in her tight clutched hand. She said "Oh" in an expiring sigh and then "Oh" again as he pulled her in close and his chin pushed her cheek around gently. They were both smiling just faintly and she was frowning too as the inch between them melted into darkness.

When they were apart she shook her head still but more in wonder than in denial. It came like this then, it was your own fault, how far back, when was the moment. It came like this and every instant the burden of tearing herself away from them together, from it, was heavier and more unimaginable. He was exultant; she resented and could not blame him but she would not be part of his exultation for it was a defeat. So far it was a defeat. And then she thought that if she stopped it being a defeat, broke off and went inside, it was still not a victory. Then it was just nothing.

"This was not my idea," she said. "Not at all my idea."

"Can I come in?"

"Oh no—no."

"Then let's jump in the car and drive somewhere."

With relief she caught at the exact phrasing—to get away from here immediately, that was accomplishment or sounded like one—as if she were fleeing from the spot of a crime. Then they were in the car going down hill with the breeze cool in their faces and she came slowly to herself. Now it was all clear in black and white.

"We'll go back to your house on the beach," she said.

"Back there?"

"Yes—we'll go back to your house. Don't let's talk. I just want to ride."

Section 14 (Part iii)

When they got to the coast again the sky was grey and at Santa Monica a sudden gust of rain bounced over them. Stahr halted beside the road, put on a raincoat and lifted the canvas top. "We've got a roof," he said.

The windshield wiper ticked domestically as a grandfather clock. Sullen cars were leaving the wet beaches and starting back into the city. Further on they ran into fog—the road lost its boundaries on either side and the lights of cars coming toward them were stationary until just before they flared past.

They had left a part of themselves behind, and they felt light and free in the car. Fog fizzed in at a chink and Kathleen took off the rose-and-blue hat in a calm, slow way that made him watch tensely, and put it under a strip of canvas in the back seat. She shook out her hair and, when she saw that Stahr was looking at her, she smiled.

The trained seal's restaurant was only a sheen of light off toward the ocean. Stahr cranked down a window and looked for landmarks but after a few more miles the fog fell away and just ahead of them the road turned off that led to his house. Out here a moon showed behind the clouds. There was still a shifting light over the sea.

The house had dissolved a little back into its elements. They found the dripping beams of a doorway and groped over mysterious waist-high obstacles to the single finished room, odorous of sawdust and wet wood. When he took her in his arms they could just see each other's eyes in the half darkness. Presently his raincoat dropped to the floor.

"Wait," she said.

She needed a minute. She did not see how any good could come from this and though this did not prevent her from being happy and desirous she needed a minute to think how it was, to go back an hour and know how it had happened. She waited in his arms, moving her head a little from side to side as she had before, only more slowly, and never taking her eyes from his. Then she discovered that he was trembling.

He discovered it at the same time and his arms relaxed. Immediately she spoke to him coarsely and provocatively and pulled his face down to hers. Then, with her knees she struggled out of something, still standing up and holding him with one arm, and kicked it off beside the coat. He was not trembling now and he held her again as they knelt down together and slid to the raincoat on the floor.

Afterwards they lay without speaking and then he was full of such tender love for her that he held her tight till a stitch tore in her dress. The small sound brought them to reality.

"I'll help you up," he said, taking her hands.

"Not just yet. I was thinking of something."

She lay in the darkness thinking irrationally that it would be such a bright, indefatigable baby, but presently she let him help her up. . . . When she came back into the room, the room was lit from a single electric fixture.

"A one-bulb lighting system," he said. "Shall I turn it off?"

"No. It's very nice. I want to see you."

They sat in the wooden frame of the window seat with the soles of shoes touching.

"You seem far away," she said.

"So do you."

"Are you surprised?"

"At what?"

"That we're two people again. Don't you always think—hope that you'll be one person and then find you're still two?"

"I feel very close to you."

"So do I to you," she said.

"Thank you."

"Thank *you*."

They laughed.

"Is this what you wanted?" she asked. "I mean last night."

"Not consciously."

"I wonder when it was settled," she brooded. "There's a moment when you needn't and then there's another moment when you know nothing in the world could keep it from happening."

This had an experienced ring and to his surprise he liked her even more. In his mood which was passionately to repeat yet not recapitulate the past it was right that it should be that way.

"I *am* rather a trollop," she said following his thoughts. "I suppose that's why I didn't get on to Edna."

"Who is Edna?"

"The girl you thought was me. The one you phoned to—who lived across the road. She's moved to Santa Barbara."

"You mean she was a tart?"

"So it seems. She went to what you call call-houses."

"That's funny."

"If she had been English I'd have known right away. But she seemed like everyone else. She only told me just before she went away."

He saw her shiver and got up, putting the raincoat around her shoulders. He opened a closet and a pile of pillows and beach mattresses fell out on the floor. There was a box of candles and he lit them around the room, attaching the electric heater where the bulb had been.

"Why was Edna afraid of me?" he asked suddenly.

"Because you were a producer. She had some awful experience or a friend of hers did. Also I think she was extremely stupid."

"How did you happen to know her?"

"She came over. Maybe she thought I was a fallen sister. She seemed quite pleasant. She said 'Call me Edna' all the time. 'Please call me Edna'—so finally I called her Edna and we were friends."

She got off the window seat so he could lay pillows along it and behind her.

"What can I do?" she said. "I'm a parasite."

"No, you're not." He put his arms around her. "Be still. Get warm."

They sat for a while quiet.

"I know why you liked me at first," she said. "Edna told me."

"What did she tell you?"

"That I looked like—Minna Davis. Several people have told me that."

He leaned away from her and nodded.

"It's here," she said, putting her hands on her cheekbones and distorting her cheeks slightly. "Here and here."

"Yes," said Stahr. "It was very strange. You look more like she actually *look*ed than how she was on the screen."

She got up, changing the subject with her gesture as if she were afraid of it.

"I'm warm now," she said. She went to the closet and peered in, came back wearing a little apron with a crystalline pattern like a snowfall. She stared around critically.

"Of course we've just moved in," she said, "—and there's a sort of echo."

She opened the door of the verandah and pulled in two wicker chairs, drying them off. He watched her move, intently yet half afraid that her body would fail somewhere and break the spell. He had watched women in screen tests and seen their beauty vanish second by second as if a lovely statue had begun to walk with meagre joints of a paper doll. But Kathleen was ruggedly set on the balls of her feet—the fragility was, as it should be, an illusion.

"It's stopped raining," she said. "It rained the day I came. Such an awful rain—so loud—like horses weeing."

He laughed.

"You'll like it. Especially if you've got to stay here. Are you going to stay here? Can't you tell me now? What's the mystery?"

She shook her head.

"Not now—it's not worth telling."

"Come here then."

She came over and stood near him and he pressed his cheek against the cool fabric of the apron.

"You're a tired man," she said putting her hand in his hair.

"Not that way."

"I didn't mean that way," she said hastily. "I meant you'll work yourself sick."

"Don't be a mother," he said.

"All right. What shall I be?"

Be a trollop, he thought. He wanted the pattern of his life broken. If he was going to die soon, like the two doctors said, he wanted to stop being Stahr for a while and hunt for love like men who had no gifts to give, like young nameless men who looked along the streets in the dark.

"You've taken off my apron," she said gently.

"Yes."

"Would anyone be passing along the beach? Shall we put out the candles?"

"No, don't put out the candles."

Afterwards she lay half on a white cushion and smiled up at him.

"I feel like Venus on the half shell," she said.

"What made you think of that?"

"Look at me. Isn't it Botticelli?"

"I don't know," he said smiling. "It is if you say so."

She yawned.

"I've had such a good time. And I'm very fond of you."

"You know a lot, don't you?"

"What do you mean?"

"Oh, from little things you've said. Or perhaps the way you say them."

She deliberated.

"Not much," she said. "I never went to a university if that's what you mean. But the man I told you about knew everything and he had a passion for educating me. He made out schedules and made me take courses at the Sorbonne and go to museums. I picked up a little."

"What was he?"

"He was a painter of sorts and a hell-cat. And a lot besides. He wanted me to read Spengler—everything was for that. All the history and philosphy and harmony was all so I could read Spengler and then I left him before we got to Spengler. At the end I think that was the chief reason he didn't want me to go."

"Who was Spengler?"

"I tell you we didn't get to him," she laughed. "And now I'm forgetting everything very patiently because it isn't likely I'll ever meet anyone like him again."

"Oh, but you shouldn't forget it," said Stahr shocked. He had an intense respect for learning, a racial memory of the old shuls. "You shouldn't forget."

"It was just in place of babies."

"You could teach your babies," he said.

"Could I?"

"Sure you could. You could give it to them while they were young. When I want to know anything I've got to ask some drunken writer. Don't throw it away."

"All right," she said getting up, "I'll tell it to my children. But it's so endless—the more you know the more there is just beyond and it keeps on coming. This man could have been anything if he hadn't been a coward and a fool."

"But you were in love with him."

"Oh yes—with all my heart." She looked through the window, shading her eyes. "It's light out there. Let's go down to the beach."

He jumped up exclaiming:

"Why, I think it's the grunion!"

"What?"

"It's tonight. It's in all the papers." He hurried out the door and she heard him open the door of the car. Presently he returned with a newspaper.

"It's at ten-sixteen. That's five minutes."

"An eclipse or something?"

"Very punctual fish," he said. "Leave your shoes and stockings and come with me."

It was a fine blue night. The tide was at the turn and the little silver fish rocked off shore waiting for 10:16. A few seconds after the time they came swarming in with the tide and Stahr and Kathleen stepped over them barefoot as they flicked slip-slop in the sand. A Negro man came along the shore toward them collecting the grunion quickly like twigs into two pails. They came in twos and threes and platoons and companies, relentless and exalted and scornful around the great bare feet of the intruders, as they had come before Sir Francis Drake had nailed his plaque to the boulder on the shore.

"I wish for another pail," the Negro man said, resting a moment.

"You've come a long way out," said Stahr.

"I used to go to Malibu but they don't like it those moving picture people."

A wave came in and forced them back, receded swiftly leaving the sand alive again.

"Is it worth the trip?" Stahr asked.

"I don't figure it that way. I really come out to read some Emerson. Have you ever read him?"

"I have," said Kathleen. "Some."

"I've got him inside my shirt. I got some Rosicrucian literature with me too but I'm fed up with them."

The wind had changed a little—the waves were stronger further down and they walked along the foaming edge of the water.

"What's your work?" the Negro asked Stahr.

"I work for the pictures."

"Oh." After a moment he added, "I never go to movies."

"Why not?" asked Stahr sharply.

"There's no profit. I never let my children go."

Stahr watched him and Kathleen watched Stahr protectively.

"Some of them are good," she said, against a wave of spray, but he did not hear her. She felt she could contradict him and said it again and this time he looked at her indifferently.

"Are the Rosicrucian brotherhood against pictures?" asked Stahr.

"Seems as if they don't know what they *are* for. One week they for one thing and next week for another."

Only the little fish were certain. Half an hour had gone and still they came. The Negro's two pails were full and finally he went off over the beach toward the road, unaware that he had rocked an industry.

Stahr and Kathleen walked back to the house and she thought how to drive his momentary blues away.

"Poor old Sambo," she said.

"What?"

"Don't you call them poor old Sambo?"

"We don't call them anything especially." After a moment he said, "They have pictures of their own."

In the house she drew on her shoes and stockings before the heater.

"I like California better," she said deliberately. "I think I was a bit sex-starved."

"That wasn't quite all was it?"

"You know it wasn't."

"It's nice to be near you."

She gave a little sigh as she stood up so small that he did not notice it.

"I don't want to lose you now," he said. "I don't know what you think of me or whether you think of me at all. As you've probably guessed my heart's in the grave—" He hesitated, wondering if this was quite true, "—but you're the most attractive woman I've met since I don't know when. I can't stop looking at you. I don't know now exactly the color of your eyes but they make me sorry for everyone in the world—"

"Stop it, stop it!" she cried laughing. "You'll have me looking in the mirror for weeks. My eyes aren't any color—they're just eyes to see with and I'm just as ordinary as I can be. I have nice teeth for an English girl—"

"You have beautiful teeth."

"—but I couldn't hold a candle to these girls I see here—"

"*You* stop it," he said. "What I said is true and I'm a cautious man."

She stood motionless a moment—thinking. She looked at him, then she looked back into herself, then at him again—then she gave up her thought.

"We must go," she said.

Now they were different people as they started back. Four times they had driven along the shore road today, each time a different pair. Curiosity, sadness and desire were behind them now; this was a true returning—to themselves and all their past and future and the encroaching presence of tomorrow. He asked her to sit close in the car and she did but they did not seem close because for that you have to seem to be growing closer. Nothing stands still. It was on his tongue to ask her to come to the house he rented and sleep there tonight—but he felt that it would make him sound lonely. As the car climbed the hill to her house Kathleen looked for something behind the seat cushion.

"What have you lost?"

"It might have fallen out," she said, feeling through her purse in the darkness.

"What was it?"

"An envelope."

"Was it important?"

"No."

But when they got to her house and Stahr turned on the dashboard light she helped take the cushions out and look again.

"It doesn't matter," she said as they walked to the door. "What's your address where you really live?"

"Just Bel-Air. There's no number."

"Where is Bel-Air?"

"It's a sort of development near Santa Monica. But you'd better call me at the studio."

"All right . . . good night, Mr. Stahr."

"*Mis*ter Stahr," he repeated, astonished.

She corrected herself gently.

"Well then, good night, Stahr. Is that better?"

He felt as though he had been pushed away a little.

"As you like," he said. He refused to let the aloofness communicate itself. He kept looking at her and moved his head from side to side in her own gesture, saying without words "you know what's happened to me." She sighed. Then she came into his arms and for a moment was his again completely. Before anything could change Stahr whispered good night and turned away and went to his car.

Winding down the hill he listened inside himself as if something by an unknown composer, powerful and strange and strong, was about to be played for the first time. The theme would be stated presently but because the composer was always new, he would not recognize it as the theme right away. It would come in some such guise as the auto-horns from the technicolor boulevards below or be barely audible, a tattoo on the muffled drum of the moon. He strained to hear it, knowing only that music was beginning, new music that he liked and did not understand. It was hard to react to what one could entirely compass—this was new and confusing, nothing one could shut off in the middle and supply the rest from an old score.

Also, and persistently, and bound up with the other, there was the Negro on the sand. He was waiting at home for Stahr with his pails of silver fish, and he would be waiting at the studio in the morning. He had said that he did not allow his children to listen to Stahr's story. He was prejudiced and wrong and he must be shown somehow, some way. A picture, many pictures, a decade of pictures, must be made to show him he was wrong. Since he had spoken, Stahr had thrown four pictures out of his plans—one that was going into production this week. They were borderline pictures in point of interest but at least he submitted the borderline pictures to the Negro and found them trash. And he put back on his list a difficult picture that he had tossed to the wolves, to Brady and Marcus and the rest, to get his way on something else. He rescued it for the Negro man.

When he drove up to his door the porch lights went on and his Filipino came down the steps to put away the car. In the library Stahr found a list of phone calls.

La Borwits
Marcus
Harlow
Rienmund
Fairbanks
Brady
Colman
Skouras
Flieshacker

The Filipino came into the room with a letter.
"This fell out of the car," he said.

"Thanks," said Stahr, "I was looking for it."

"Will you be running a picture tonight, Mr. Stahr?"

"No thanks—you can go to bed."

The letter, to his surprise, was addressed to Monroe Stahr, Esq. He started to open it—then it occurred to him that she had wanted to recapture it, and possibly to withdraw it. If she had had a phone he would have called her for permission before opening it. He held it for a moment. It had been written before they met—it was odd to think that whatever it said was now invalidated; it possessed the interest of a souvenir by representing a mood that was gone.

Still he did not like to read it without asking her. He put it down beside a pile of scripts and sat down with the top script in his lap. He was proud of resisting his first impulse to open the letter. It seemed to prove that he was not "losing his head." He had never lost his head about Minna even in the beginning—it had been the most appropriate and regal match imaginable. She had loved him always and just before she died all unwilling and surprised his tenderness had burst and surged toward her and he had been in love with her. In love with Minna and death together—with the world into which she looked so alone that he wanted to go with her there.

But "falling for dames" had never been an obsession—his brother had gone to pieces over a dame, or rather over dame after dame after dame. But Stahr, in his younger days, had them once and never more than once—like one drink. He had quite another sort of adventure reserved for his mind—something better than a series of emotional sprees. Like many brilliant men he had grown up dead cold. Beginning at about twelve probably with the total rejection common to those of extraordinary mental powers, the "see here—this is all wrong—a mess—all a lie—and a sham—" he swept it all away, everything, as men of his type do and then instead of being a son-of-a-bitch as most of them are he looked around at the barrenness that was left and said to himself "*This* will never do." And so he had learned tolerance, kindness, forbearance, and even affection like lessons.

The Filipino boy brought in a carafe of water and bowls of nuts and fruit and said good night. Stahr opened the first script and began to read.

He read for three hours—stopping from time to time, editing without a pencil. Sometimes he looked up, warm from some vague happy thought that was not in the script, and it took him a minute each time to remember what it was. Then he knew it was Kathleen and looked at the letter—it was nice to have a letter.

It was three o'clock when a vein began to bump in the back of his hand signalling that it was time to quit. Kathleen was really far away now with the waning night—the different aspects of her telescoped into the memory of a single thrilling stranger bound to him only by a few slender hours. It seemed perfectly all right to open the letter.

Dear Mr. Stahr:

In half an hour I will be keeping my date with you. When we say good bye I will hand you this letter. It is to tell you that I am to be married soon and that I won't be able to see you after today.

I should have told you last night but it didn't seem to concern you. And it would seem silly to spend this beautiful afternoon telling you about it and watching your interest fade. Let it fade all at once—now. I will have told you enough to convince you that I am Nobody's Prize Potato. (I have just learned that expression—from my hostess of last night who called and stayed an hour. She seems to believe that everyone is Nobody's Prize Potato—except you. I think I am supposed to tell you she thinks this, so give her a job if you can.)

I am very flattered that anyone who sees so many lovely women I can't finish this sentence but you know what I mean. And I will be late if I don't go to meet you right now.

> *With All Good Wishes*
> *Kathleen Moore.*

Stahr's first feeling was like fear; his first thought was that the letter was invalidated—she had even tried to retrieve it. But then he remembered "Mister Stahr" just at the end, and that she had asked him his address—she had probably already written him another letter, which would also say good bye. Illogically he was shocked by the letter's indifference to what had happened later. He read it again realizing that it foresaw nothing. Yet in front of the house she had decided to let it stand, belittling everything that had happened, curving her mind away from the fact that there had been no other man in her consciousness that afternoon. But he could not even believe this now and the whole adventure began to peel away even as he recapitualted it searchingly to himself. The car, the hill, the hat, the music, the letter itself blew off like the scraps of tar paper from the rubble of his house. And Kathleen departed, packing up her remembered gestures, her softly moving head, her sturdy eager body, her bare feet in the wet swirling sand. The skies paled and faded—the wind and rain turned dreary, washing the silver fish back to sea. It was only one more day, and nothing was left except the pile of scripts upon the table.

He went upstairs. Minna died again on the first landing and he forgot her lingeringly and miserably again, step by step to the top. The empty floor stretched around him—the doors with no one sleeping behind. In his room Stahr took off his tie, untied his shoes and sat on the side of his bed. It was all closed out except for something that he could not remember; then he remembered, her car was still down in the parking lot of the hotel. He set his clock to give him six hours' sleep.

Section 15 (first part)

This is Cecelia taking up the story. I think it would be most interesting to follow my own movements at this point, as this is a time in my life that I am ashamed of. What people are ashamed of usually makes a good story.

When I sent Wylie White over to Martha Dodd's table he had no success in finding out who the girl was, but it had suddenly become my chief interest in life. Also I guessed—correctly—that it would be Martha Dodd's: to have had at your table a girl who is admired by royalty, who may be tagged for a coronet in our little feudal system—and not even know her name.

I had only a speaking acquaintance with Martha and it would be too obvious to approach her directly, but I went out to the studio Monday and dropped in on Rose Meloney.

Rose Meloney was quite a friend of mine. I thought of her rather as a child thinks of a family dependent. I knew she was a writer but I grew up thinking that writer and secretary were the same except that a writer usually smelled of cocktails and came more often to meals. They were spoken of the same way when they were not around—except for a species called playwrights who came from the East. These were treated with respect if they did not stay long—if they did they sank with the others into the white collar class.

Rose's office was in the "old writers' building." There was one on every lot, a row of iron maidens left over from silent days and still resounding the dull moans of cloistered hacks and bums. There was the story of the new producer who had gone down the line one day and then reported excitedly to the head office.

"Who are those men?"

"They're supposed to be writers."

"I thought so. Well, I watched them for ten minutes and there were two of them that didn't write a line."

Rose was at her typewriter about to break off for lunch. I told her frankly that I had a rival.

"It's a dark horse," I said. "I can't even find out her name."

"Oh," said Rose. "Well, maybe I know something about that. I heard something from somebody."

The somebody, of course, was her nephew Ned Sollinger, Stahr's office boy. He had been her pride and hope. She had sent him through New York University where he played on the football team. Then in his first year at medical school after a girl turned him down he dissected out the least publicized section of a lady corpse and sent it to the girl. Don't ask me why. In disgrace with fortune and men's eyes he had begun life at the bottom again, and was still there.

"What do you know?" I asked.

"It was the night of the earthquake. She fell into the lake on the back lot and he dove in and saved her life. Someone else told me it was his balcony she jumped off of and broke her arm."

"Who was she?"

"Well, that's funny too—"

Her phone rang and I waited restlessly during a long conversation she had with Joe Rienmund. He seemed to be trying to find out over the phone how good she was or whether she had ever written any pictures at all. And she was reputed to have been on the set the day Griffith invented the close-up! While he talked she groaned silently, writhed, made faces into the receiver, held it all in her lap so that the voice reached her faintly—and kept up a side chatter to me.

"What is *he* doing—killing time between appontments? . . . He's asked me every one of these questions ten times . . . that's all on a memorandum I sent him. . . ."

And into the phone:

"If this goes up to Monroe it won't be my doing. I want to go right through to the end."

She shut her eyes in agony again.

"Now he's casting it . . . he's casting the minor characters . . . he's going to have Buddy Ebsen. . . . My God he just hasn't anything to do . . . now he's on Harry Davenport—he means Donald Crisp . . . he's got a big casting directory open in his lap and I can hear him turn the pages . . . he's a big important man this morning, a second Stahr, and for Christ sake I've got two scenes to do before lunch."

Rienmund quit finally or was interrupted at his end. A waiter came in from the commissary with Rose's luncheon and a Coca-Cola for me—I wasn't lunching that summer. Rose wrote down one sentence on her typewriter before she ate. It interested me the way she wrote. One day I was there when she and a young man had just lifted a story out of "The Saturday Evening Post"—changing the characters and all. Then they began to write it making each line answer the line before it, and of course it sounded just like people do in life when they're straining to be anything—funny or gentle or brave. I always wanted to see that one on the screen but I missed it somehow.

I found her as lovable as a cheap old toy. She made three thousand a week, and her husbands all drank and beat her nearly to death. But today I had an axe to grind.

"You don't know her name?" I persisted.

"Oh—" said Rose "—*that*. Well, he kept calling her up afterwards and he told Katy Doolan it was the wrong name after all."

"I think he found her," I said. "Do you know Martha Dodd?"

"Hasn't that little girl had a tough break though!" she exclaimed with ready theatrical sympathy.

"Could you possibly invite her to lunch tomorrow?"

"Oh, I think she gets enough to eat all right. There's a Mexican—"

I explained that my motives were not charitable. Rose agreed to cooperate. She called Martha Dodd.

15 (second part)

We had lunch next day at the Bev Brown Derby, a languid restaurant patronized for its food by clients who always look as if they'd like to lie down. There is some animation at lunch where the women put on a show for the first five minutes after they eat but we were a tepid threesome. I should have come right out with my curiosity. Martha Dodd was an agricultural girl who had never quite understood what had happened to her and had nothing to show for it except a washed out look about the eyes. She still believed that the life she had tasted was reality and this was only a long waiting.

"I had a beautiful place in 1928," she told us. "Thirty acres, with a miniature golf course and a pool and a gorgeous view. All spring I was up to my ass in daisies."

I ended by asking her to come over and meet Father. This was pure penance for having had "a mixed motive" and being ashamed of it. One doesn't mix motives in Hollywood—it is confusing. Everybody understands, and the climate wears you down. A mixed motive is conspicuous waste.

Rose left us at the studio gate, disgusted by my cowardice. Martha had worked up inside to a pitch about her career—not a very high pitch because of seven years of neglect but a sort of nervous acquiescence and I was going to speak strongly to Father. They never did anything for people like Martha who had made them so much money at one time. They let them slip away into misery eked out with extra work—it would have been kinder to ship them out of town. And Father was being so proud of me this summer. I had to keep him from telling everybody just how I was brought up to produce such a perfect jewel. And Bennington—oh what an exclusive—dear God my heart. I assured him there was the usual proportion of natural born skivies and biddies tastefully concealed by throw overs from Sex, Fifth Avenue; but Father had worked himself up to practically an alumnus. "You've had everything," he used to say happily. Everything included roughly the two years in Florence where I managed against heavy odds to be the only virgin in school, and the courtesy debut in Boston, Massachusetts. I was a veritable flower of the fine old cost-and-gross aristocracy.

So I knew he would do something for Martha Dodd and as we went into his office I had great dreams of doing something for Johnny Swanson the cowboy too and Evelyn Brent and all sorts of discarded flowers. Father was a charming and sympathetic man—except for that time I had seen him unexpectedly in New York—and there was something touching about his being my father. After all he was *my* father—he would do anything in the world for me.

Only Rosemary Schmiel was in the outer office and she was on Birdy Peters' phone. She waved for me to sit down but I was full of my plans and telling Martha to take it easy I pressed the clicker under Rosemary's desk and went toward the opened door.

"Your father's in conference," Rosemary called. "Not in conference but I ought to—"

By this time I was through the door and a little vestibule and another door and caught Father in his shirt sleeves, very sweaty and trying to open a window. It was a hot day but I hadn't realized it was that hot and thought he was ill.

"No, I'm all right," he said. "What is it?"

I told him. I told him the whole theory of people like Martha Dodd, walking up and down his office. How he could use them and guarantee them regular employment. He seemed to take me up excitedly and kept nodding and agreeing, and I felt closer to him than I had for a long time. I came close and kissed him on his cheek. He was trembling and his shirt was soaked through.

"You're not well," I said. "Or you're in some sort of stew."

"No, I'm not at all."

"What is it?"

"Oh it's Monroe," he said. "That God damn little Vine Street Jesus! He's in my hair night and day!"

"What's happened?" I asked, very much cooler.

"Oh, he sits like a little God damn priest or rabbi and says what he'll do and he won't do. I can't tell you now—I'm half crazy. Why don't you go along."

"I won't have you like this."

"Go along I tell you!" I sniffed but he never drank.

"Go and brush your hair," I said. "I want you to see Martha Dodd."

"In here! I'd never get rid of her."

"Out there then. Go wash up first. Put on another shirt."

With an exaggerated gesture of despair he went into the little bathroom adjoining. It was hot in the office as if it had been closed for hours and maybe that was making him sick so I opened two more windows.

"You go along," Father called from behind the closed door of the bathroom. "I'll be there presently."

"Be awfully nice to her," I said. "No charity."

As if it were Martha speaking for herself a long low moan came from somewhere in the room. I was startled—then transfixed as it came again not from the bathroom where Father was, not from outside but from a closet in the wall across from me. How I was brave enough I don't know but I ran across to it and opened it and Father's secretary Birdy Peters tumbled out stark naked—just like a corpse in the movies. With her came a gust of stifling, stuffy air. She flopped sideways on the floor with the one hand still clutching some clothes and lay on the floor bathed in sweat—just as Father came in from the bathroom. I could feel him standing behind me and without turning I knew exactly how he looked, for I had surprised him before.

"Cover her up," I said, covering her up myself with a rug from the couch. "Cover her *up*!"

I left the office. Rosemary Schmiel saw my face as I came out and responded with a terrified expression. I never saw her again or Birdy Peters either. As Martha and I went out Martha asked

"What's the matter dear?"—and when I didn't say anything, "You did your best. Probably it was the wrong time. I'll tell you what I'll do. I'll take you to see a very nice English girl. Did you see the girl that Stahr danced with at our table the other night?"

So at the price of a little immersion in the family drains I had what I wanted.

I don't remember much about our call. She wasn't at home was one reason. The screen door of her house was unlocked and Martha went in calling "Kathleen" with bright familiarity. The room we saw was bare and formal as a hotel; there were flowers about but they did not look like sent flowers. Also Martha found a note on the table which said, "Leave the dress. Have gone looking for a job. Will drop by tomorrow."

Martha read it twice but it didn't seem to be for Stahr, and we waited five minutes. People's houses are very still when they are gone. Not that I expect them to be jumping around but I leave the observation for what it's worth. Very still. Prim almost with just a fly holding down the place and paying no attention to you, and the corner of a curtain blowing.

"I wonder what kind of a job," said Martha. "Last Sunday she went somewhere with Stahr."

But I was no longer interested. It seemed awful to be here—producer's blood, I thought in horror. And in quick panic I pulled her out into the placid sunshine. It was no use—I felt just black and awful. I had always been proud of my body—I had a way of thinking of it as geometric which made everything it did seem all right and there was probably not any kind of place, including churches and offices and shrines, where people had not embraced—but no one had ever stuffed me naked into a hole in the wall in the middle of a business day.

Episode 16, First Part

"If you were in a drug store," said Stahr "—having a prescription filled—"

"You mean a chemist?" Boxley asked.

"If you were in a chemist's," conceded Stahr, "and you were getting a prescription for some member of your family who was very sick—"

"—Very ill?" queried Boxley.

"Very ill. *Then* whatever caught your attention through the window, whatever distracted you and held you would probably be material for pictures."

"A murder outside the window, you mean."

"There you go," said Stahr smiling. "It might be a spider working on the pane."

"Of course—I see."

"I'm afraid you don't, Mr. Boxley. You see it for *your* medium but not for ours. You keep the spiders for yourself and you try to pin the murders on us."

"I might as well leave," said Boxley. "I'm no good to you. I've been here three weeks and I've accomplished nothing. I make suggestions but no one writes them down."

"I want you to stay. Something in you doesn't like pictures, doesn't like telling a story this way—"

"It's such a damned bother," exploded Boxley. "You can't let yourself go—"

He checked himself. He knew that Stahr, the helmsman, was finding time for him in the middle of a constant stiff blow—that they were talking in the always creaking rigging of a ship sailing in great awkward tacks along an open sea. Or else—it seemed at times—they were in a huge quarry where even the newly cut marble bore the tracery of old pediments, half obliterated inscriptions of the past.

"I keep wishing you could start over," Boxley said. "It's this mass production."

"That's the condition," said Stahr. "There's always some lousy condition. We're making a life of Rubens—suppose I asked you to do portraits of rich dopes like Pat Brady and me and Gary Cooper and Marcus when you wanted to paint Jesus Christ! Wouldn't you feel you had a condition? Our condition is that we have to take people's own favorite folklore and dress it up and give it back to them. Anything beyond that is sugar. So won't you give us some sugar, Mr. Boxley?"

Boxley knew he could sit with Wylie White tonight at the Troc raging at Stahr, but he had been reading Lord Charnwood and he recognized that Stahr like Lincoln was a leader carrying on a long war on many fronts; almost single-handed he had moved pictures sharply forward through a decade, to a point where the content of the "A productions" was wider and richer than that of the stage. Stahr was an artist only as Mr. Lincoln was a general, perforce and as a layman.

"Come down to La Borwits' office with me," said Stahr. "They sure need some sugar there."

In La Borwits' office two writers, a shorthand secretary and a supervisor sat in a tense smokey stalemate where Stahr had left them three hours before. He looked at the faces one after another and found nothing. La Borwits spoke with awed reverence for his defeat.

"We've just got too many characters, Monroe."

Stahr snorted affably.

"That's the principal idea of the picture."

He took some change out of his pocket, looked up at the suspended light and tossed up half a dollar which clanked into the bowl. He looked at the coins in his hands and selected a quarter.

La Borwits watched miserably; he knew this was a favorite idea of Stahr's and he saw the sands running out. At the moment everyone's back was toward him. Suddenly he brought up his hands from their placid position under the desk and threw them high in the air, so high that they seemed to leave his wrists—and then he caught them neatly as they were descending. After that he felt better. He was in control.

One of the writers had taken out some coins also and presently rules were defined. "You have to toss your coin through the chains without hitting them. Whatever falls into the light is the kitty."

They played for half an hour—all except Boxley who sat aside and dug into the script, and the secretary who kept tally. She calculated the cost of the four men's time, arriving at a figure of

sixteen hundred dollars. At the end La Borwits was winner by
$5.50 and a janitor brought in a step-ladder to take the money out
of the light.

Boxley spoke up suddenly.

"You have the stuffings of a tuhkey here," he said.

"What!"

"It's not pictures."

They looked at him in astonishment. Stahr concealed a smile.

"So we've got a real picture man here!" exclaimed La Borwits.

"A lot of beautiful speeches," said Boxley boldly. "But no situations. After all, you know, it's not going to be a novel: and it's too
long. I can't exactly describe how I feel but it's not quite right. And
it leaves me cold."

He was giving them back what had been handed him for three
weeks. Stahr turned away, watching the others out of the corner of
his eye.

"We don't need *less* characters," said Boxley. "We need *more*. As
I see it that's the idea."

"That's the idea," said the writers.

"Yes—that's the idea," said La Borwits.

Boxley was inspired by the attention he had created.

"Let each character see himself in the other's place," he said.
"The policeman is about to arrest the thief when he sees that the
thief actually has *his* face. I mean show it that way. You could
almost call the thing 'Put Yourself in My Place.' "

Suddenly they were at work again—taking up this new theme in
turn like hepcats in a swing band and going to town with it. They
might throw it out again tomorrow but life had come back for a
moment. Pitching the coins had done it as much as Boxley. Stahr
had recreated the proper atmosphere—never consenting to be a
driver of the driven, but feeling like and acting like and sometimes
even looking like a small boy getting up a show.

He left them, touching Boxley on the shoulder in passing—a
deliberate accolade—he didn't want them to gang up on him and
break his spirit in an hour.

Episode 16 (Part 2)

Doctor Baer was waiting in his inner office. With him was a colored man with a portable cardiograph like a huge suitcase. Stahr called it the lie detector. He stripped to the waist and the weekly examination began.

"How've you been feeling?"

"Oh—the usual," said Stahr.

"Been hard at it? Getting any sleep?"

"No—about five hours. If I go to bed early I just lie there."

"Take the sleeping pills."

"The yellow one gives me a hangover."

"Take two red ones then."

"That's a nightmare."

"Take one of each—the yellow first."

"All right—I'll try. How've *you* been?"

"Say—I take care of myself, Monroe. I save myself."

"The hell you do—you're up all night sometimes."

"Then I sleep all next day."

After ten minutes Baer said:

"Seems O.K. The blood pressure's up five points."

"Good," said Stahr. "That's good isn't it?"

"That's good. I'll develop the cardiograms tonight. When are you coming away with me?"

"Oh, some time," said Stahr lightly. "In about six weeks things'll ease up."

Baer looked at him with a genuine looking that had grown over three years.

"You got better in thirty-three when you laid up," he said. "Even for three weeks."

"I will again."

No he wouldn't, Baer thought. With Minna's help he had enforced a few short rests years ago and lately he had hinted around trying to find who Stahr considered his closest friends. Who could take him away and keep him away. It would almost surely be useless. He was due to die very soon now. Within six months one could say definitely. What was the use of developing the cardiograms? You couldn't persuade a man like Stahr to stop and lie down and look at the sky for six months. He would much rather die. He said differently but what it added up to was the definite urge toward total exhaustion that he had run into before. Fatigue was a drug as well as a poison and Stahr apparently derived some rare almost physical pleasure from working lightheaded with weariness. It was a perversion of the life force he had seen before but he had almost stopped trying to interfere with it. He had cured a man or so—a hollow triumph of killing and preserving the shell.

"You hold your own," he said.

They exchanged a glance. Did Stahr know? Probably. But he did not know when—he did not know how soon now.

"If I hold my own I can't ask more," said Stahr.

The colored man had finished packing the apparatus.

"Next week same time?"

"O.K., Bill," said Stahr. "Good bye."

As the door closed Stahr switched open the Dictograph. Miss Doolan's voice came through immediately.

"Do you know a Miss Kathleen Moore?"

"What do you mean?" he asked startled.

"A Miss Kathleen Moore is on the line. She said you asked her to call."

"Well, my God!" he exclaimed. He was swept with indignant rapture. It had been five days—this would never do at all.

"She's on now?"

"Yes."

"Well, all right then."

In a moment he heard the voice up close to him.

"Are you married?" he asked, low and surly.

"No, not yet."

His memory blocked out her face and form—as he sat down she seemed to lean down to his desk keeping level with his eyes.

"What's on your mind?" he asked in the same surly voice. It was hard to talk that way.

"You did find the letter?" she asked.

"Yes. It turned up that night."

"That's what I want to speak to you about."

He found an attitude at length—he was outraged.

"What is there to talk about?" he demanded.

"I tried to write you another letter but it wouldn't write."

"I know that too."

There was a pause.

"Oh cheer up!" she said surprisingly. "This doesn't sound like you. It *is* Stahr, isn't it? That very nice Mr. Stahr?"

"I feel a little outraged," he said almost pompously. "I don't see the use of this. I had at least a pleasant memory of you."

"I don't believe it's you," she said. "Next thing you'll wish me luck." Suddenly she laughed. "Is this what you planned to say? I know how *aw*ful it gets when you plan to say anything—"

"I never expected to hear from you again," he said with dignity; but it was no use, she laughed again—a woman's laugh that is like a child's, just one syllable, a crow and a cry of delight.

"Do you know how you make me feel?" she demanded. "Like one day in London during a caterpillar plague when a hot furry thing dropped in my mouth."

"I'm sorry."

"Oh please wake up," she begged. "I want to see you. I can't explain things on the phone. It was no fun for me either, you understand."

"I'm very busy. There's a sneak preview in Glendale tonight."

"Is that an invitation?"

"George Boxley, the English writer, is going with me." He surprised himself. "Do you want to come along?"

"How could we talk?"

She considered. "Why don't you call for me afterwards," she suggested. "We could ride around."

Miss Doolan on the huge Dictograph was trying to cut in a shooting director—the only interruption ever permitted. He flipped the button and called "wait" impatiently into the machine.

"About eleven?" Kathleen was saying confidently.

The idea of "Riding around" seemed so unwise that if he could have thought of the words to refuse her he would have spoken them but he did not want to be the caterpillar. Suddenly he had no attitude left except the sense that the day, at least, was complete. It had an evening—a beginning, a middle and an end.

He rapped on the screen door, heard her call from inside, and stood waiting where the level fell away. From below came the whir of a lawn mower—a man was cutting his grass at midnight. The moon was so bright that Stahr could see him plainly a hundred feet off and down as he stopped and rested on the handle before pushing it back across his garden. There was a midsummer restlessness abroad—early August with imprudent loves and impulsive crimes. With little more to expect from summer one tried anxiously to live in the present—or, if there was no present, to invent one.

She came at last. She was all different and delighted. She wore a suit with a skirt that she kept hitching up as they walked down to the car with a brave gay, stimulating reckless air of "Tighten up your belt, baby. Let's get going—to any pole." Stahr had brought his limousine with the chauffeur, and the intimacy of the four walls whisking them along a new curve in the dark took away any strangeness at once. In its way the little trip they made was one of the best times he had ever had in life. It was certainly one of the times when, if he knew he was going to die, it was not tonight.

She told him her story. She sat beside him cool and gleaming for a while, spinning on excitedly, carrying him to far places with her, meeting and knowing the people she had known. The story was vague at first. "This Man" was the one she had loved and lived with. "This American" was the one who had rescued her when she was sinking into a quicksand.

"Who is he—the American?"

Oh, names—what did they matter? No one important like Stahr, not rich. He had lived in London and now they would live out here. She was going to be a good wife, a real person. He was getting a divorce—not just on account of her—but that was the delay.

"But the first man?" asked Stahr. "How did you get into that?"

Oh, that was a blessing at first. From sixteen to twenty-one the thing was to eat. The day her stepmother presented her at Court they had one shilling to eat with so as not to feel faint. Sixpence apiece but the stepmother watched while she ate. After a few months the stepmother died and she would have sold out for that shilling but she was too weak to go into the streets. London can be harsh—oh quite.

Was there nobody?

There were friends in Ireland who sent butter. There was a soup kitchen. There was a visit to an uncle who made advances to her when she had a full stomach, and she held out and got fifty pounds out of him for not telling his wife.

"Couldn't you work?" Stahr asked.

"I worked. I sold cars. Once I sold a car."

"But couldn't you get a regular job?"

"It's hard—it's different. There was a feeling that people like me forced other people out of jobs. A woman struck me when I tried to get a job as chambermaid in a hotel."

"But you were presented at Court?"

"That was my stepmother who did that—on an off chance. I was nobody. My father was shot by the Black and Tans in twenty-two when I was a child. He wrote a book called 'Last Blessing.' Did you ever read it?"

"I don't read."

"I wish you'd buy it for the movies. It's a good little book. I still get a royalty from it—ten shillings a year."

Then she met "The Man" and they travelled the world around. She had been to all the places that Stahr made movies of, and lived in cities whose names he had never heard. Then The Man went to seed, drinking and sleeping with the housemaids and trying to force her off on his friends. They all tried to make her stick with him. They said she had saved him and should cleave to him longer now, indefinitely, to the end. It was her duty. They brought enormous pressure to bear. But she had met The American, and so finally she ran away.

"You should have run away before."

"Well, you see it was difficult." She hesitated, and plunged. "You see I ran away from a king."

His moralities somehow collapsed—she had managed to top him. A confusion of thoughts raced through his head—one of them a faint old credo that all royalty was diseased.

"It wasn't the King of England," she said. "My king was out of job as he used to say. There are lots of kings in London." She laughed—then added almost defiantly, "He was very attractive until he began drinking and raising hell."

"What was he king of?"

She told him—and Stahr visualized the face out of old newsreels.

"He was a very learned man," she said. "He could have taught all sorts of subjects. But he wasn't much like a king. Not nearly as much as you. None of them were."

This time Stahr laughed.

"They were the standard article," he said.

"You know what I mean. They all felt old fashioned. Most of them tried so hard to keep up with things. They were always advised to keep up with things. One was a Syndicalist for instance. And one used to carry around a couple of clippings about a tennis tournament when he was in the semi-finals. I saw those clippings a dozen times."

They rode through Griffith Park and out past the dark studios of Burbank, past the airports and along the way to Pasadena past the neon signs of roadside cabarets. Up in his head he wanted her but it was late and just the ride was an overwhelming joy. They held hands and once she came close in to his arms saying, "Oh you're *so* nice. I *do* like to be with you." But her mind was divided—this was not his night as the Sunday afternoon had been his. She was absorbed in herself, stung into excitement by telling of her own adventures; he could not help wondering if he was getting the story she had saved up for The American.

"How long have you known The American?" he asked.

"Oh I knew him for several months. We used to meet. We understand each other. He used to say 'It looks like a cinch from now on.' "

"Then why did you call me up?"

She hesitated.

"I wanted to see you once more. Then too—he was supposed to arrive today but last night he wired that he'd be another week. I wanted to talk to a friend—after all you *are* my friend."

He wanted her very much now but one part of his mind was cold and kept saying: she wants to see if I'm in love with her, if I want to marry her. Then she'd consider whether or not to throw this man over. She won't consider it till I've committed myself.

"Are you in love with The American?" he asked.

"Oh yes. It's absolutely arranged. He saved my life and my reason. He's moving half way around the world for me. I insisted on that."

"But are you in love with him?"

"Oh yes, I'm in love with him."

The "Oh yes" told him she was not—told him to speak for himself—that she would see. He took her in his arms and kissed her deliberately on the mouth and held her for a long time. It was so warm.

"Not tonight," she whispered.

"All right."

They passed over suicide bridge with the high new wire.

"I know what it is," she said, "but how stupid. English people don't kill themselves when they don't get what they want."

They turned around in the driveway of a hotel and started back. It was a dark night with no moon. The wave of desire had passed and neither spoke for a while. Her talk of kings had carried him oddly back in flashes to the pearly White Way of Main Street in Erie, Pennsylvania when he was fifteen. There was a restaurant with lobsters in the window and green weeds and bright light on a shell cavern and behind a red curtain the terribly strange brooding mystery of people and violin music. That was just before he left for New York. This girl reminded him of the fresh iced fish and lobsters in the window. She was Beautiful Doll. Minna had never been Beautiful Doll.

They looked at each other and her eyes asked "Shall I marry The American?" He did not answer. After a while he said:

"Let's go somewhere for the week-end."

She considered.

"Are you talking about tomorrow?"

"I'm afraid I am."

"Well, I'll tell you tomorrow," she said.

"Tell me tonight. I'd be afraid—"

"—find a note in the car?" she laughed. "No there's no note in the car. You know almost everything now."

"Almost everything."

"Yes—almost. A few little things."

He would have to know what they were. She would tell him tomorrow. He doubted—or he wanted to doubt—if there had been a maze of philandering—a fixation had held her to The Man, the king, firmly and long. Three years of a highly anomalous position—one foot in the Palace and one in the background. "You had to laugh a lot," she said. "I learned to laugh a lot."

"He could have married you—like Mrs. Simpson," Stahr said in protest.

"Oh, he was married. And he wasn't a romantic." She stopped herself.

"Am I?"

"Yes," she said unwillingly, as if she were laying down a trump. "Part of you is. You're three or four different men but each of them out in the open. Like all Americans."

"Don't start trusting Americans too implicitly," he said, smiling. "They may be out in the open but they change very fast."

She looked concerned.

"Do they?"

"Very fast and all at once," he said. "And nothing ever changes them back."

"You frighten me. I always had a great sense of security with Americans."

She seemed suddenly so alone that he took her hand.

"Where will we go tomorrow?" he said. "Maybe up in the mountains. I've got everything to do tomorrow but I won't do any of it. We can start at four and get there by afternoon."

"I'm not sure. I seem to be a little mixed up. This doesn't seem to be quite the girl who came out to California for a new life."

He could have said it then, said "It is a new life" for he knew it was, he knew he could not let her go now, but something else said to sleep on it as an adult, no romantic. And tell her tomorrow. Still she was looking at him her eyes wandering from his forehead to his chin and back again, and then up and down once more with that odd slowly waving motion of her head.

. . . It is your chance, Stahr. Better take it now. This is your girl. She can save you, she can worry you back to life. She will take looking after and you will grow strong to do it. But take her now—tell her and take her away. Neither of you knows it but far away over the night The American has changed his plans. At this moment his train is speeding through Albuquerque; the schedule is accurate. The engineer is on time. In the morning he will be here.

. . . The chauffeur turned up the hill to Kathleen's house. It seemed warm even in darkness—wherever he had been near her was by way of being enchanted place for Stahr: this limousine—the rising house at the beach, the very distances they had already covered together over the sprawled city. The hill they climbed now gave forth a sort of glow, a sustained sound that struck his soul alert with delight.

As he said good bye he felt again that it was impossible to leave her, even for a few hours. There was only ten years between them but he felt that madness about it akin to the love of an ageing man for a young girl. It was a deep and desperate time-need, a clock ticking with his heart, and it urged him against the whole logic of his life to walk past her into the house now—and say "This is forever."

Kathleen waited, irresolute herself—pink and silver frost waiting to melt with spring. She was a European, humble in the face of power, but there was a fierce self-respect that would only let her go so far. She had no illusions about the considerations that swayed princes.

"We'll go to the mountains tomorrow," said Stahr. Many thousands of people depended on his balanced judgement—you can suddenly blunt a quality you have lived by for twenty years.

He was very busy the next morning, Saturday. At two o'clock when he came from luncheon there was a stack of telegrams—a company ship was lost in the Arctic, a star was in disgrace, a writer was sueing for one million dollars, Jews were dead miserably beyond the sea. The last telegram stared up at him:

I WAS MARRIED AT NOON TODAY GOODBYE, and on a sticker attached *Send your answer by Western Union Telegram*.

Episode 17

I knew nothing about any of this. I went up to Lake Louise and when I came back didn't go near the studio. I think I would have started East in mid-August—if Stahr hadn't called me up one day at home.

"I want you to arrange something, Cecelia—I want to meet a Communist Party member."

"Which one?" I asked, somewhat startled.

"Any one."

"Haven't you got plenty out there?"

"I mean one of their organizers—from New York."

The summer before I had been all politics—I could probably have arranged a meeting with Harry Bridges. But my boy had been killed in an auto accident after I went back to college and I was out of touch with such things. I had heard there was a man from "The New Masses" around somewhere.

"Will you promise him immunity?" I asked, joking.

"Oh yes," Stahr answered seriously. "I won't hurt him. Get one that can talk—tell him to bring one of his books along."

He spoke as if he wanted to meet a member of the "I AM" cult.

"Do you want a blonde, or a brunette?"

"Oh, get a man," he said hastily.

Hearing Stahr's voice cheered me up—since I barged in on Father it had all seemed a paddling about in thin spittle. Stahr changed everything about it—changed the angle from which I saw it, changed the very air. He was like a brazier out of doors on a cool night.

"I don't think your father ought to know," he said. "Can we pretend the man is a Bulgarian musician or something?"

"Oh, they don't dress up any more," I said.

It was harder to arrange than I thought—Stahr's negotiations with the Writers Guild, which had continued over a year, were approaching a dead end. Perhaps they were afraid of being corrupted, and I was asked what Stahr's "proposition" was. Afterwards Stahr told me that he prepared for the meeting by running off the Russian Revolutionary Films that he had in his film library at home. He also ran off "Doctor Caligari" and Salvador Dali's "Un Chien Andalou," possibly suspecting that they had a bearing on the matter. He had been startled by the Russian Films back in the twenties and on Wylie White's suggestion he had had the script department get him up a two-page "treatment" of the "Communist Manifesto."

But his mind was closed on the subject. He was a rationalist who did his own reasoning without benefit of books—and he had just managed to climb out of a thousand years of Jewry into the late eighteenth century. He could not bear to see it melt away—he cherished the parvenu's passionate loyalty to an imaginary past.

The meeting took place in what I called the "processed leather room"—it was one of six done for us by a decorator from Sloane's years ago, and the term stuck in my head. It was *the* most decorator's room—an angora wool carpet the color of dawn, the most delicate grey imaginable—you hardly dared walk on it; and the silver panelling and leather tables and creamy pictures and slim fragilities looked so easy to stain that we could not breathe hard in there, though it was wonderful to look into from the door when the windows were open and the curtains whimpered querulously against the breeze. It was a lineal descendant of the old American parlor that used to be closed except on Sunday. But it was exactly the room for the occasion and I hoped that whatever happened would give it character and make it henceforth part of our house.

Stahr arrived first. He was white and nervous and troubled —except for his voice which was always quiet and full of consideration. There was a brave personal quality in the way he would meet you—he would walk right up to you and put aside something that was in the way, and grow to know you all over as if he couldn't help himself. I kissed him for some reason, and took him into the processed leather room.

"When do you go back to college?" he asked.

We had been over this fascinating ground before.

"Would you like me if I were a little shorter?" I asked. "I could wear low heels and plaster down my hair."

"Let's have dinner tonight," he suggested. "People will think I'm your father but I don't mind."

"I *love* old men," I assured him. "Unless the man has a crutch I feel it's just a boy and girl affair."

"Have you had many of those?"

"Enough."

"People fall in and out of love all the time, don't they."

"Every three years so Fanny Brice says. I just read it in the paper."

"I wonder how they manage it," he said. "I know it's true because I see them. But they look so con*vinced* every time. And then suddenly they don't look convinced. But they get convinced all over."

"You've been making too many movies."

"I wonder if they're as convinced the second time or the third time or the fourth time," he persisted.

"More each time," I said. "Most of all the last time."

He thought this over and seemed to agree.

"I suppose so. Most of all the last time."

I didn't like the way he said this and I suddenly saw that under the surface he was miserable.

"It's a great nuisance," he said. "It'll be better when it's over."

"Wait a *min*ute! Perhaps pictures are in the wrong hands."

Brimmer, the Party Member, was announced and going to meet him I slid over to the door on one of those gossamer throw-rugs and practically into his arms.

He was a nice-looking man, this Brimmer—a little on the order of Spencer Tracy but with a stronger face and a wider range of reactions written up in it. I couldn't help thinking as he and Stahr smiled and shook hands and squared off, that they were two of the most alert men I had ever seen. They were very conscious of each other immediately—both as polite to me as you please but with a softening of the ends of their sentences when they turned in my direction.

"What are you people trying to do?" demanded Stahr. "You've got my young men all upset."

"That keeps them awake, doesn't it?" said Brimmer.

"First we let half a dozen Russians study the plant," said Stahr. "As a model plant, you understand. And then you try to break up the unity that makes it a model plant."

"The unity?" Brimmer repeated. "Do you mean what's known as the company spirit?"

"Oh, not that," said Stahr, impatiently. "It seems to be *me* you're after. Last week a writer came into my office—a drunk—a man who's been floating around for years just two steps out of the bughouse—and began telling me my business."

Brimmer smiled.

"You don't look to me like a man who could be told his business, Mr. Stahr."

They would both have tea. When I came back Stahr was telling a story about the Warner brothers and Brimmer was laughing with him.

"I'll tell you another one," Stahr said. "Balanchine the Russian dancer had them mixed up with the Ritz Brothers. He didn't know which ones he was training and which ones he was working for. He used to go around saying 'I cannot train those Warner Brothers to dance.' "

It looked like a quiet afternoon. Brimmer asked him why the producers didn't back the Anti-Nazi League.

"Because of you people," said Stahr. "It's your way of getting at the writers. In the long view you're wasting your time. Writers are children—even in normal times they can't keep their minds on their work."

"They're the farmers in this business," said Brimmer pleasantly. "They grow the grain but they're not in at the feast. Their feeling toward the producer is like the farmers' resentment of the city fellow."

I was wondering about Stahr's girl—whether it was all over between them. Later when I heard the whole thing from Kathleen, standing in the rain in a wretched road called Goldwyn Terrace, I figured out that this must have been a week after she sent him the telegram. She couldn't help the telegram. The man got off the train unexpectedly and walked her to the registry office without a flicker of doubt that this was what she wanted. It was eight in the morning and Kathleen was in such a daze that she was chiefly concerned in how to get the telegram to Stahr. In theory you could stop and say "Listen I forgot to tell you but I met a man." But this track had been laid down so thoroughly, with such confidence, such struggle, such relief that when it came along suddenly cutting across the other she found herself on it like a car on a closed switch. He watched her write the telegram, looking directly at it across the table, and she hoped he couldn't read upside down. . . .

When my mind came back into the room they had destroyed the poor writers—Brimmer had gone so far as to admit they were "unstable."

"They are not equipped for authority," said Stahr. "There is no substitute for will. Sometimes you have to fake will when you don't feel it at all."

"I've had that experience."

"You have to say 'It's got to be like this—no other way'—even if you're not sure. A dozen times a week that happens to me. Situations where there is no real reason for anything. You pretend there is."

"All leaders have felt that," said Brimmer. "Labor leaders, and certainly military leaders."

"So I've had to take an attitude in this Guild matter. It looks to me like a try for power and all I am going to give the writers is money."

"You give some of them very little money. Thirty dollars a week."

"Who gets that?" asked Stahr surprised.

"The ones who are commodities and easy to replace."

"Not on my lot," said Stahr.

"Oh yes," said Brimmer. "Two men in your shorts department get thirty dollars a week."

"Who?"

"Man named Ransome—man named O'Brien."

Stahr and I smiled together.

"Those are not writers," said Stahr. "Those are cousins of Cecelia's father."

"There are some in other studios," said Brimmer.

Stahr took his teaspoon and poured himself some medicine from a little bottle.

"What's a fink?" he asked suddenly.

"A fink? That's a strike breaker or a Company Tec."

"I thought so," said Stahr. "I've got a fifteen hundred dollar writer that every time he walks through the commissary keeps saying 'Fink!' behind other writers' chairs. If he didn't scare hell out of them it'd be funny."

Brimmer laughed.

"I'd like to see that," he said.

"You wouldn't like to spend a day with me over there?" suggested Stahr.

Brimmer laughed with genuine amusement.

"No, Mr. Stahr. But I don't doubt but that I'd be impressed. I've heard you're one of the hardest working and most efficient men in the entire West. It'd be a privilege to watch you but I'm afraid I'll have to deny myself."

Stahr looked at me.

"I like your friend," he said. "He's crazy but I like him." He looked closely at Brimmer. "Born on this side?"

"Oh yes. Several generations."

"Many of them like you?"

"My father was a Baptist minister."

"I mean are many of the Reds. I'd like to meet this big Jew that tried to blow over the Ford factory. What's his name—"

"Frankensteen?"

"That's the man. I guess some of you believe in it."

"Quite a few," said Brimmer dryly.

"Not you," said Stahr.

A shade of annoyance floated across Brimmer's face.

"Oh yes," he said.

"Oh no," said Stahr. "Maybe you did once."

Brimmer shrugged his shoulders.

"Perhaps the boot's on the other foot," he said. "At the bottom of your heart, Mr. Stahr, you know I'm right."

"No," said Stahr, "I think it's a bunch of tripe."

"—you think to yourself 'He's right' but you think the system will last out your time."

"You don't really think you're going to overthrow the government."

"No, Mr. Stahr. But we think perhaps you are."

They were nicking at each other—little pricking strokes like men do sometimes. Women do it too but it is a joined battle then with no quarter, but it is not pleasant to watch men do it because you never know what's next. Certainly it wasn't improving the tonal associations of the room for me and I moved them out the French window into our golden-yellow California garden.

It was midsummer but fresh water from the gasping sprinklers made the lawn glitter like spring. I could see Brimmer look at it with a sigh in his glance—a way they have. He opened up big outside—inches taller than I thought and broad-shouldered. He reminded me a little of Superman when he takes off his spectacles. I thought he was as attractive as men can be who don't really care about women as such. We played a round robin game of ping-pong and he handled his bat well. I heard Father come into the house singing that damn "Little Man, You've Had a Busy Day" and then breaking off as if he remembered we weren't speaking any more. It was half past six—my car was standing in the drive and I suggested we go down to the Trocadero for dinner.

Brimmer had that look that Father O'Ney had that time in New York when he turned his collar around and went with Father and me to the Russian Ballet. He hadn't quite ought to be here. When Bernie the photographer, who was waiting there for some big game or other, came up to our table he looked trapped—Stahr made Bernie go away, and I would like to have had the picture.

Then, to my astonishment, Stahr had three cocktails one after the other.

"Now I know you've been disappointed in love," I said.

"What makes you think that, Cecelia?"

"Cocktails."

"Oh, I never drink, Cecelia. I get dyspepsia—I never have been tight."

I counted them. "—two—*three*."

"I didn't realize. I couldn't taste them. I thought there was something the matter."

A silly glassy look darted into his eye—then passed away.

"This is my first drink in a week," said Brimmer. "I did my drinking in the navy."

The look was back in Stahr's eye—he winked it fatuously at me and said:

"This soapbox son-of-a-bitch has been working on the navy."

Brimmer didn't know quite how to take this. Evidently he decided to include it with the evening for he smiled faintly and I saw Stahr was smiling too. I was relieved when I saw it was safely in the great American tradition and I tried to take hold of the conversation but Stahr seemed suddenly all right.

"Here's my typical experience," he said very succinctly and clearly to Brimmer. "The best director in Hollywood—a man I never interfere with—has some streak in him that wants to slip a pansy into every picture or something on that order. Something offensive. He stamps it in deep like a watermark so I can't get it out. Every time he does it the Legion of Decency moves a step forward and something has to be sacrificed out of some honest film."

"Typical organization trouble," agreed Brimmer.

"Typical," said Stahr. "It's an endless battle. So now this director tells me it's all right because he's got a Directors Guild and I can't oppress the poor. That's how you add to my troubles."

"It's a little remote from us," said Brimmer smiling. "I don't think we'd make much headway with the directors."

"The directors used to be my pals," said Stahr proudly.

It was like Edward the VII's boast that he had moved in the best society in Europe.

"But some of them have never forgiven me," he continued, "—for bringing out stage directors when sound came in. It put them on their toes and made them learn their jobs all over but they never did really forgive me. That time we imported a whole new hogshead full of writers and I thought they were great fellows till they all went Red."

Gary Cooper came in and sat down in a corner with a bunch of men who breathed whenever he did and looked as if they lived off him and weren't budging an inch. A woman across the room looked around and turned out to be Carole Lombard—I was glad that Brimmer was at least getting an eyeful.

Stahr ordered a whiskey and soda and, almost immediately, another. He ate nothing but a few spoonfuls of soup and he said all the awful things about everybody being lazy so-and-so's and none of it mattered to *him* because he had lots of money—it was the kind of talk you heard whenever Father and his friends were together. I think Stahr realized that it sounded pretty ugly outside of the proper company—maybe he had never heard how it sounded before. Anyhow he shut up and drank off a cup of black coffee. I loved him and what he said didn't change that but I hated Brimmer to carry off this impression. I wanted him to see Stahr as a sort of technological virtuoso and here Stahr had been playing the wicked overseer to a point he would have called trash if he had watched it on the screen.

"I'm a production man," he said as if to modify his previous attitude. "I like writers—I think I understand them. I don't want to kick anybody out if they do their work."

"We don't want you to," said Brimmer pleasantly. "We'd like to take you over as a going concern."

Stahr nodded grimly.

"I'd like to put you in a roomful of my partners. They've all got a dozen reasons for having Fitts run you fellows out of town."

"We appreciate your protection," said Brimmer with a certain irony. "Frankly we *do* find you difficult, Mr. Stahr—precisely because you are a paternalistic employer and your influence is very great."

Stahr was only half listening.

"I never thought," he said, "—that I had more brains than a writer has. But I always thought that his brains be*longed* to me— because I knew how to use them. Like the Romans—I've heard that they never invented things but they knew what to do with them. Do you see? I don't say it's right. But it's the way I've always felt—since I was a boy."

This interested Brimmer—the first thing that had interested him for an hour.

"You know yourself very well, Mr. Stahr," he said.

I think he wanted to get away. He had been curious to see what kind of man Stahr was and now he thought he knew. Still hoping things would be different I rashly urged him to ride home with us but when Stahr stopped by the bar for another drink I knew I'd made a mistake.

It was a gentle, harmless, motionless evening with a lot of Saturday cars. Stahr's hand lay along the back of the seat touching my hair. Suddenly I wished it had been about ten years ago. I would have been nine. Brimmer about eighteen and working his way through some mid-western college and Stahr twenty-five just having inherited the world and full of confidence and joy. We would both have looked up to Stahr so, without question. And here we were in an adult conflict to which there was no peaceable solution, complicated now with exhaustion and drink.

We turned in at our drive and I drove around to the garden again.

"I must go along now," said Brimmer. "I've got to meet some people."

"No, stay," said Stahr. "I never have said what I wanted. We'll play ping-pong and have another drink and then we'll tear into each other."

Brimmer hesitated. Stahr turned on the floodlight and picked up his ping-pong bat and I went into the house for some whiskey—I wouldn't have dared disobey him.

When I came back they were not playing but Stahr was batting a whole box of new balls across to Brimmer who turned them aside. When I arrived he quit and took the bottle and retired to a chair just out of the floodlight, watching in dark dangerous majesty. He was pale—he was so transparent that you could almost watch the alcohol mingle with the poison of his exhaustion.

"Time to relax on Saturday night," he said.

"You're not relaxing," I said.

He was carrying on a losing battle with his instinct toward schizophrenia.

"I'm going to beat up Brimmer," he announced after a moment. "I'm going to handle this thing personally."

"Can't you pay somebody to do it?" asked Brimmer.

I signalled him to keep quiet.

"I do my own dirty work," said Stahr. "I'm going to beat hell out of you and put you on a train."

He got up and came forward and I put my arms around him, gripping him.

"Please *stop* this!" I said. "Oh, you're being so bad."

"This fellow has an influence over you," he said darkly. "Over all you young people. You don't know what you're doing."

"Please go home," I said to Brimmer.

Stahr's suit was made of slippery cloth and suddenly he slipped away from me and went for Brimmer. Brimmer retreated backward around the table. There was an odd expression in his face and afterwards I thought it looked as if he were saying, "Is *this* all? This frail half sick *person* holding up the whole thing."

Then Stahr came close, his hands going up. It seemed to me that Brimmer held him off with his left arm a minute and then I looked away—I couldn't bear to watch.

When I looked back Stahr was out of sight below the level of the table and Brimmer was looking down at him.

"Please go home," I said to Brimmer.

"All right." He stood looking down at Stahr as I came around the table. "I always wanted to hit ten million dollars but I didn't know it would be like this."

Stahr lay motionless.

"Please go," I said.

"I'm sorry. Can I help—"

"No. Please go. I understand."

He looked again, a little awed at the depths of Stahr's repose which he had created in a split second. Then he went quickly away over the grass and I knelt down and shook Stahr. In a moment he came awake with a terrific convulsion and bounced up on his feet.

"Where is he?" he shouted.

"Who?" I asked innocently.

"That American. Why in hell did you have to marry him, you damn fool."

"Monroe—he's gone. I didn't marry anybody."

I pushed him down in a chair.

"He's been gone half an hour," I lied.

The ping-pong balls lay around in the grass like a constellation of stars. I turned on a sprinkler and came back with a wet handkerchief but there was no mark on Stahr—he must have been hit in the side of the head. He went off behind some trees and was sick and I heard him kicking up some earth over it. After that he seemed all right but he wouldn't go into the house till I got him some mouthwash so I took back the whiskey bottle and got a mouthwash bottle. His wretched essay at getting drunk was over. I've been out with college freshmen but for sheer ineptitude and absence of the Bacchic spirit it unquestionably took the cake. Every bad thing happened to him but that was all.

We went in the house; the cook said Father and Mr. Marcus and Flieshacker were on the verandah so we stayed in the "processed leather room." We both sat down in a couple of places and seemed to slide off and finally I sat on a fur rug and Stahr on a footstool beside me.

"Did I hit him?" he asked.

"Oh, yes," I said. "Quite badly."

"I don't believe it." After a minute he added, "I didn't want to hurt him. I just wanted to chase him out. I guess he got scared and hit me."

If this was his interpretation of what had happened it was all right with me.

"Do you hold it against him?"

"Oh no," he said. "I was drunk." He looked around. "I've never been in here before—who did this room—somebody from the studio?"

"Somebody from New York."

"Well, I'll have to get you out of here," he said in his old pleasant way. "How would you like to go out to Doug Fairbanks' ranch and spend the night? He asked me—I know he'd love to have you."

That's how the two weeks started that he and I went around together. It only took one of them for Louella to have us married.

SELECTED FITZGERALD
WORKING NOTES

F. Scott Fitzgerald accumulated more material than he could incorporate in *The Love of the Last Tycoon*.

The Princeton University Library holds more than two-hundred pages of Fitzgerald's notes covering the gestation and composition of the novel: character lists, character sketches, outlines of action, plot ideas, dialogue, description, strippings from short stories, notes on Irving Thalberg and MGM, background on the movie industry and the Writers Guild, and marked typescripts of posthumously published Hollywood stories ("Last Kiss" and "Director's Special"). Most of the pages are in typescript and were either typed from Fitzgerald's manuscript notes or dictated by him. The pages are undated, and they have been reshuffled whenever a researcher has handled them. The specimen notes have been selected and ordered by the editor: planning memos are followed by work-in-progress or writing notes. The rationale for selection was to include notes that reveal Fitzgerald's thinking about the evolving novel.

Query—where is the man for these 3 weeks. Getting his divorce.

Query—why does Thalia after meeting a man of great power, and falling for him violently so that she sleeps with him then marry another man?

Answer—she actually knows Stahr only a week after she falls in love with him and during that time resolutely considers it as a romance *just as he does*. In fact the letter impells the phone and the seduction is a surprise.

Even so why does she not now stop the other thing? Ans.—Some pure circumstance intervenes—Stahr's moral doubts about her are a factor that let him neglect her at one important moment, his work keeps him from calling her. The moment it is too late he is desperate.

Plant his anonymity—his many plans. Your contributions can't be measured. They have to pay in statue. On his deathbed that haunts him. Maybe a statue.

I must not alienate the reader from her at the beginning, but must give the feeling that "well, I don't like this girl much, but I am going to stick around

A brilliant producer, Staler, has everything, but has lost his wife whom he loved. He meets her image, falls for her, finding in mid-channel that he is breaking up a good marriage.

He leaves her, takes up with another girl and is plunged into a growing row in his business which gets worse and finally strikes him down in Washington. On his return his ambitious pardner has done some dirty tricks. Staler calls him and in his disgust throws over the man's daughter, returns to the girl and tries for a divorce.

His enemy strikes by going to the jealous husband. Staler takes counter-measures then seeing it makes him as low as what he is fighting he gives up and goes away — with no future that he sees. The plane falls.

Bradogue and Stahr are actually great friends but
Bradogue ~~wants him~~ out — Schwartz tries to
warn him. Stahr meets the English wife
of a cutter and is haunted by her. He meets
her half secretly at the football — everywhere
except at his office. There is absolutely no
privacy and the seduction finally takes place at
Malibu in his unfurnished house.

Cecilia knows all this and it breaks her heart. But
nobody knows, including her, who the girl really is.
She ~~inadvertently~~ tells her father who discovers who the girl is
and immediately sees his chance — he goes to Stahr,
~~threatening~~ him in a pleasant way and suggesting he marry
Cecilia but Stahr counters with what he knows about
Bradogue (the affair of the girls husband murdered — Stahr has
found it out from his wifes trained nurse whom he did)
Stahrs problem is whether to quit or go on in the
face of inevitable discovery. He and Thalia are taking
breathless chances. Now the storm breaks and everyone he had
counted on turns against him. He plays with the idea of
marrying Cecilia as the best way of getting out and is seen
everywhere with her. The reds see him as a conservative — Wall
Street as a red. He has one last fling with Thalia, tells Cecilia
about it — throws her over and goes to Washington where he falls
sick with worry.

Meanwhile Bradogue gets the news to the cutter who has
long ~~suspected~~ something. Robinson (who is Savoy) feels it's
the perfect anti-semetic smear gets backing and prepares the
boat.

Knowing nothing of this Stahr gets word of the salary cuts and
comes west sick. Thalia gets word to him. He goes to work and
crushes the whole thing by doing just what Bradogue did — plan to have
Robinson killed. The clock has gone around. He leaves Hollywood
plan alibi — in the air he decides against it. The plane falls.
Thalia is ruined. She never went inside a studio.

Characters

(1) Monroe Stahr

(2) Thalia Smith

(3) Major Billy Baird

(4) Cecilia Baird

(5) W. Bronson Smith

Maude ⎱ Secretaries
Polly ⎰

Wylie White

Lois-on-the-head-of-Siva?

Mortimer Fleishacker

Hedda or Luella

David Stahr

Liz anyhow from another tangle.

Director Jack Kincaid
(Cooper - Holden - Wellman)

Dotty in Hollywood

Johnny Swanson
(Harry Carey)

Manny Schwartze

Lee Spurgeon (Welford Beaton)

Double Talk Mike Van Dyke

Robinson (Covering)

Rogers — writer.

Alec Milkhaus, Camera Man

Washington Doctors

Jesus Rogueriquez, actor

Chinese Actress

Trocadero Doorman

Sarah ⎱
Molly ⎰ Actresses
Daisy

The Skouras Brothers

The Communist

The Pilot ——— Wilkerson

The Williams Boy

Georges Gralboered

Sch[l]chgd of Notre Dame

Locations (another Page) ~~enclosed~~ Drugstore, Races, Potomar

MUST REDUCE CHARACTERS

Monroe Stahr
Major Pat Brady
W. Bronson Smith
Wylie White
Jaques La Borwits (change)
Rienmund
John Broaca - director
Manny Schwartz
Boxley
Johnny Swanson
   (Harry Carey)   *Greek*
Pedro Garcia, Camera Man (~~new~~ name)
Robinson (Lovering)
Washington Doctors
Prince Agge - guest (change name)
              Early fascist
Mike Van Dyke - Double Talk (guest)
Marquands (writers) guests
The Skouras Brothers (new name) guests
The Communist (quiet kid) guest
The Pilot (guest)
The Williams Boy (guest)
Publicity Man (guest)
Mort Flieshacker, Company Lawyer (guest) *Change name.*
Mr. Marcus (is Marcus Loew dead?) guest
Leanbaum (Rapf)(guest)
The Star
"Red" Ridingwood (director)

Thalia Smith
Cecelia Brady
Catherine Doolan, Stahr's
    first secretary
Rose Meloney
Edna
Hedda or Louella (guest)
Liz anyhow from another
    angle (guest)
Dotty in Hollywood (guest)
Birdy Peters)
Maude   ) Brady's
Rosemary Schmiel) secretaries
Chinese Actress (guest)
Sarah)
Molly) Actresses (guests)
Daisy)
Bitch

The Hollywood producers have not had
the early advantages which are considered standard —
and it is not very kindly nor
Christian to mock at them. ~~But they say~~
~~low grade men are such delusion~~ they'ar
~~delusionedly low~~ ~~accept mockery~~
~~and hatred as their share and it~~
~~to it our grows to meet able comes &~~
~~not consider them~~ as less than
less than people & I have never heard a writer or
play route or an actress or a novelist
say a nice thing about a producer ~~except~~
possibly the one ~~it was~~ the one at the moment
working for ~~them~~ — from Dorothy
Parkers exhibit who was "only a
ponys bottom" — on up. They ~~cannot~~ is to a much
~~be pleasant~~ to ask that they have pleasant natures
for it is a filthy job to debauch
a nation — even though the nation wallows
in the spew.

~~On~~ their side they have their
money and their ~~strident~~ molls and

They accept mockery and hatred
as their share. They do not mind —
They link it up with the oppressions
visited upon their parents in
Oddessa and Loty — they are
having their moment among the
fleshpots before returning to the
darker and bloodier ghettos that
lie ahead.

and see what she has to say because she has let drop a few things that make me think that given the right circumstances she might have been worthwhile."

Nevertheless, the first episode must close with something definitely arresting or shocking about herself.

———

Action is character.

Consider transferring strong scenes to rear.

———

Cannot the characters express themselves more—I mean psychologically, not didactically.

———

When he came down out of the sky he saw the Glendale airport below him, bright, warm. The moon was straight ahead above the Pacific that was the lands of the Long Beach Naval Reserves; further down there was Huntington Park and on the right, the great mutual blur of Santa Monica. Stahr loves these clusters of lights as if they were something he had set up himself as an electrician. "And this I shall black-out, and this I will lay my hand on, reluctantly, cruelly, definitely, and squeeze and squeeze, and squeeze, and something dark, something I don't know—something I may have left behind me in the dark. But these lights, this brightness, these clusters of human hope, of wild desire—I shall takes these lights in my fingers. I shall make them bright, and whether they shine or not, it is these fingers that they shall succeed or fail."
The plane bumped lower, lower; the engines stopped breathing—then round softly and down. It was always very exciting to get there.

Important that he knew the business side first. His submission of a scenario was probably a very quaking venture on his part—very timorous. He must have had no more aesthetic education after finishing secondary school than I did. He had to pick the whole thing up out of the air not even by reading though probably he did some—still in all he probably learned pictures from pictures and naturally got his sense of realities from acute observation and men. He was therefore as unliterate a man as you can imagine in regard to formative influence.

———

I want to write scenes that are frightening and inimitable. I don't want to be as intelligible to my contemporaries as Ernest who as Gertrude Stein said, is bound for the Museums. I am sure I am far enough ahead to have some small immortality if I can keep well.

———

Cecelia does not tell the story though I write it as if she does whenever I can get the effect of looking out.

———

While he was on the make Stahr was as shrewd, ruthless, and opportunistic as the next man, but he arrived quickly after only a short breathless struggle, and once arrived he found it easier to be fair and generous and honorable than not to be. So he granted the premises on which he was founded — he was a better man than most of us, less bruised, less fearful, and less corrupt.

———

The morale of the studio, Stahr's morale, had survived the expansion, the arrival of sound and, up to this point, the crash and the depression. Other studios had lost identity, changed personel, changed policies, wavered in subjection to Eastern stockholders, or meekly followed the procession. But Stahr's incalculable prestige had created an optimism only equalled by that of the River Rouge plant in its great days.

———

Some of the conversation in the long day more sexy in tone. Not too much and in good taste.

———

Change Garcia to a Greek.

———

Explain his attitude towards authors and how it was like the attitude of Bernard Shaw's attitude in the preface to "Plays pleasant and unpleasant". That is, he liked them, but to some extent he saw them as a necessary evil. How thereafter, he developed the process of having the author working behind another, practically his invention; his ideas about continuity, how the links of the chain should be very closely knit rather than merely linked.

———

Tracing Stahr biologically through a day in terms of blood pressure. Did he take coffee? Was it all will? Did he rest well?

———

Affable for Stahr. Speak soft but carry a big stick.

———

How popular he was with men from the beginning in a free and easy way. There was never anything priggish or self-superiority in his casual conversation that make men uneasy in the company of other men.

———

La Borwitz. Joe Mank—pictures smell of rotten bananas.

———

The idea of a certain great film which Stahr has long planned—a very rough subject or irreligious. An original. And have the censor interfere.

———

Be sure the solution of the director incident is not too neat. Keep the coat thing but somehow remove the smarty superman element with a little irony.

———

Firing director seems a small thing to do unless someone else is scared, or director is fierce and brutal.

———

Profit-sharing contract—Important. Stahr had that sort of contract and yet did the Good Earth.

———

He was under no illusion about success—the varying components of its make up. For instance he was right a little more often than most men but this was trebly reinforced by his habit of saying things in an utterly assured way, no less forceful for being soft. He knew that the intuitional proportion of superior rightness in his thoughts was simply incalculable importance— he knew also that it might cease at any time but this was something he did not like to think about.

———

Stahr tells someone a plot half in Yiddish.

———

What is missing Ridingwood scene is imagination etc. What an extraordinary thing that it should all have been there for Ridingwood and then not there.

———

Correction: Ridingwood Sceme insert—
Ridinghood followed Stahr back across the stage, again trying to keep up again falling behind. The assistant director spoke to him. "Just hold it," Red said frowning, and six hundred thousand of dollars were immobilized—interest at twenty dollars a minute.
More here.
In the car Stahr had control of his temper. He spoke regretfully. "I'm afraid it's no go, Red. She's putting it over on you. She's loafing. It's not just my opinion."

———

Correction: Ridingwood Scene—
You didn't want to work with Lewin did you King?
I couldn't stand it Monroe.
You didn't want these scenes rewritten.
If I can have my own man. I don't want some writer like X who doesn't know his ass about pictures sit here and kibitz.
Stahr's face flexed. He reached out suddenly and tore open King's blouse the great buttons bursting off to the floor. (one button?)

———

If you think there are a lot of attractive young men around Hollywood you are wrong. There are handsome males but even when their names are Brown or Jones or Robinson they seem like the type you can find on any cheap beach in Italy. Like the oranges and lemons they are plentiful and large but they have no taste. That's why I went with Wylie White. He was a southerner and at his worst he had a code to violate. It was fun to watch him doing it.

———

This will concern itself with Cecelia's love for Stahr and the episode will concern itself with her discovery of her father.

(a) This episode begins with Cecelia taking up the story directly and describing an affair she was having with a young man. Have her describe it just as women do when they feel that they will be more convincing by telling almost everything and leaving out the main thing rather than the second method, of course, is wiser for women not to mention anything or any incident about which they are not prepared to reveal the whole truth. That is, she tells our listener, our reader, our recorder a lot about this affair which was engrossing her attention at this time, but always casually reassuring him that while there had been a lot of struggling, she had preserved her "virtue" Have her make a great emphasis on this enough so that perhaps the wisest of the readers may think "she does protest too much". Nevertheless let her in a burst of conventional self-righteousness think that she has convinced the reader that her relations with this undetermined man are essentially not most extreme. Now at this point, either by an accidental meeting on her way to see her father on the lot or perhaps because Stahr has sent for her thinking she could do something for Thalia—something he has planned for Thalia, perhaps something in the nature of a job or some sort of work that Thalia's interested in.

In the scene that takes place, she, Cecelia the narrator, should realize the depth of her love for this man at its fullest and I would like to do some very strong, quiet writing there to describe her feelings. In the writing, Cecelia should appear at her best and at her most profound. It is rather her feeling about Stahr that I want to describe than an objective picture of Stahr at this particular point. I want to find some new method of describing this. Some method in which everything that surrounds him assumes a magical touch, a magical quality without resorting to any of the old dodges of her touching the objects that he touches. I want her feelings to soar to the highest pitch of which she is capable and I want her in this episode to, for the benefit of the reader, to set away everything tawdry or superficial in her nature. This should be one of the strongest episodes in the book.

Now when the episode with Stahr is over, I want her to leave his office and have outside his office, a tremendous reaction from this exaltation and in this reaction I want her to tell the reader or the recorder the truth about the fact that she had given herself to this other man the night before—whom she has no intention of marrying, perhaps an almost experimental gesture.

———

I went to the screen actors ball. I shall not describe it. Suffice to say the lights shone over fair women and brave, not very brave men.

———

Shaken by the flare-up they go back, she still thinking she can withdraw. She could not bear to think. It was tonight. It is a murky rainy dusk, a dreary day (change former time to sunset) They left the hotel a little more than three hours ago but it seemed a long time. Get them there quickly. Odd effect of the place like a set. The mood should be two people—free— He has an overwhelming urge toward the girl who promises to give life back to him—though he has no idea yet of marriage—she is the heart of hope and freshness. *He seduces her because she is slipping away*—she lets herself be seduced because of overwhelming admiration (the phone call). Once settled it is sexual, breathless, immediate. Then gentle and tender for awhile.

———

This girl had a life—it was very seldom he met anyone whose life did not depend in some way on him or hope to depend on him.

———

I have had five tumultuous years that were about one part ecstacy to four parts misery and I want to settle down as a good wife and a real person. The man I am going to marry will never be an important man like you. We will not move in your sphere and probably it wouldn't please him to know I had gone out with such a "big shot" before he arrived. The man I am going to marry saved my reason such as it is, took me out of an impossible situation and sent me here to California.

———

Letter could be a "please-it-means-so-much-to-me-so-little-to-you." Also gratitude motif to man is left out.

———

Where will the warmth come from in this. Why does he think she's warm. Warmer than the voice in Farewell. My girls were all so warm and full of promise. The sea at night. What can I do to make it honest and different?

———

Sheilah and Frances hate the letter and both miss more emotion or something about seduction. The talk about Edna seems cold. They would like to develop negro and Stahr's reaction. They do not understand that the girl is not in the market—suspect her of leading him on. But he must not know the truth so perhaps the reader should.

———

Kathleen is physically attracted. Also playing with idea that she might marry him right away. But her debt makes her dismiss this.

———

The phone in the workman's shed actually rings and she catches a glimpse of his power which he hadn't intended. It fascinates her. He represents action. He hadn't intended to answer the phone.

———

This is Celia taking up the story. I should probably explain why I spent so much of the summer hanging around the studio. Well, for one thing I was too big to keep out now and I knew how to do it without bothering people. I had had a difference with Wylie White about who had the say about my body so there was ———, whom I didn't intend to marry who was playing the man who *al*most got the girl in three pictures at once and had to be on the lot. And thirdly, most important I had nothing else to do. (Finish with description of Hollywood boys.)

———

The Bradogue character, to be a convincing villain must, like Joe Mank— have some attractive exterior facets. The reason that louses from "Pretty Boy" Floyd all the way down to Whitney, the stockbroker have been able to get away with their chacaneries is that they have had external facets which are very pleasing so Bradogue must be a very handsome man. This attractiveness whatever it is—looks or manners—he has managed to half sell to his daughter. She knows pragmatically and by observation that he is an unscrupulous man, yet the charm must have touched her so that when she comes from Stahr's office in this exalted mood, it is half in her mind to ask her father if he thinks that Stahr will ever marry again. In other words, if she has a chance to get Stahr. (Cecelia is either divorced or motherless or has a stepmother)

Cecelia comes to her father's office full of the idea that perhaps Stahr might marry again, perhaps by some wile, from use of her youth that she could "get him," full of complete exaltation and wanting to tell her father about it simply because her father is the nearest person to her and because that charm—which I will have to create in Bradogue—has fooled her at times into thinking that he is a decent and sympathetic person and going through the outer offices (which must be very protective and elaborate—something like the entrance to the Stromberg-Hyman bungalow) she notices that one of the outside secretaries (create a minor caricature giving this girl some special characteristic)—look through list of characters—is in a state of agitation. However, it is nothing to what she finds when after pressing the secret catch to her father's office (I must interrupt by saying that the secretary has assured her that her father is not in conference and then contradicts herself and then re-contradicts herself) in which she finds her father, his coat, tie and vest are off and he is perspiring profusely and seems terrifically upset.

Cecelia is so absorbed in her story that on receiving the formal answer that "No, he is not busy, not busy at all", she launches into her own affairs and only after some moments does she perceive that her father is really in some kind of stew, made sympathetic by her own passion for Stahr, she comes close to him and starts to put her arm on his shoulder and he shrinks away from her. He launches suddenly into a tirade against Stahr which shocks her—the tirade is based perhaps on the quarrel he had with Stahr at luncheon in the commissary about making the expensive picture. In any case, it is purely a business attack upon what he considers Stahr's bogus idealism and of course has no effect on Cecelia. But the vehemence with which he talks is of the kind that if he had been a drinking man would have made her think he was drinking.

———

The break between Stahr and Thalia has been of Stahr's making. I may or may not show the scene in which this occurs, but Stahr's motive is roughly: "I am not going to marry this girl. My plans do not include marrying again. She hasn't the particular shine, glamor, poise, cultural background that would make her the fitting match for this high destiny toward which I seem to be going or this position in which I find myself; therefore, I am really indulging myself by cutting her off from Robinson who is obviously a fine fellow, who adores her and would be a good provider and a good husband."

———

At first, for some hours, *they share an overwhelming joy.* They eat together and make love, cling together at times, each cannot bear to let the other out of his sight. The reunion has been so strong in its emotional implications that it seems to the reader as well as to Stahr and Thalia that it is the prelude to an immediate marriage and almost a fade out and a happy ending. At some point though, during that same evening or perhaps the next morning which would be necessarily then a Sunday, something happens (invent some detail or small instant) which gives Stahr the idea: *After all, this is not what I intended. I didn't intend to marry this girl. It is against the logic of my life.* The premises that I set out for myself when I was young do not include this. The cold part of Stahr has crept in a little, not the cold emotion, but the cold part of his mind and almost at the instant in which he realizes and *shows it perhaps by some flicker of his expression,* Thalia who by now is as close to him as if she had lived with him for fifty years, knows it and makes up her mind what to do.

———

Final Form for the Brimmer Episode
More indication of Stahr's state. In trouble. Why he went over their heads—realizing the "little bit more" approach. Department of Justice. Sat full of promise.

———

Junior writers $300.
Minor poets—$500. a week.
Broken novelists—$850.–$1000.
One play dramatists—$1500.
Sucks—$2000. —Wits—$2500.

———

In thirty-four and thirty-five the party line crept into everything except the Sears Roebuck Catalogue.

———

Stahr as a sort of Rimbeau. Precocity and irony which is born young.

———

Stahr: Those men won't want to make good pictures after I'm gone—

———

Stahr didn't die of overwork—he died of a certain number of forces allied against him.

———

Men who have been endowed with unusual powers for work or analysis or ingredients that go to make big personal successes, seem to forget as soon as they are rich that such abilities are not evenly distributed among the other men of their kind. So when the suggestion of a Union springs out of this act of Baird's Stahr seems to reverse his form, join the other side and almost to ally himself with Baird. Note also in the epilogue that I want to show that Stahr left certain harm behind him just as he left good behind him. That some of his reactionary creations such as the Screen Playwrights existed long after his death just as so much of his valuable creative work survived him.

———

Bradogue who is great on the horses and has long rebelled against what he thinks of as Stahr's idealism and extravagance in the picture business, seeing cuts made in other industries is taking advantage of a special situation. The situation is that Stahr who is in the East has fallen ill and has succumbed to a complete nervous and physical breakdown affecting his heart so that what he thought would be a four or five day trip devoted largely to discussion with certain blocks of stockholders has become a conference around a sickbed. Stahr who has previously been in general good health, though conscious of a growing fatigue, has the natural rebellion of an active man and of what the doctor says and asks for a specialist. The specialist confirms what the doctor said and gives Stahr what amounts to an ultimatum: That is a death sentence unless he stops here and now and rests himself in some quiet way. He suggests a trip around the world or a year off or anything that will divorce him from work.

The idea fills Stahr with a horror that I must write a big scene to bring off. Such a scene as has never been written. The scene that to Stahr is the equivalent to that of an amorous man being told that he is about to be castrated. In other words, the words of the doctor fill Stahr with a horror that I must be able to convey to the laziest reader—the blow to Stahr and the utter unwillingness to admit that at this point, 35 years old, his body should refuse to serve him and carry on these plans which he has built up like a pyramid of fairy skyscrapers in his imagination.

He has survived the talkies, the depression, carried his company over terrific obstacles and done it all with a growing sense of kingliness—of some essential difference which he could not help feeling between himself and the ordinary run of man and now from the mere accident of one organ of his body refusing to pull its weight, he is incapacitated from continuing. Let him go through every stage of revolt.

Meanwhile, however, the stockholders are meeting around his bed and only by certain things that he lets slip to them does he divulge what is going on inside himself. However, enough has been divulged so that there have been telephone calls to Bradogue and Bradogue himself has gotten in touch with both doctors and in his winning way, posing as Stahr's friend, found out the truth that Stahr is definitely an unwell man. All this Cecelia finds out from her father on her return. Once again, we see Cecelia at her best, not as a very effectual character, but again as a person who under certain circumstances might have been quite a person. She tells the recorder or the reader how she got in touch with Rogers and was rather surprised to find that Rogers had been re-hired before Stahr left (she has heard, of course, about how Stahr found him in his office, in fact she has heard everything that is told in the book). Rogers knows that the whole lot is in a ferment and that various meetings are being called.

We are going to cut at this point to the meeting of camera men (cutters) at which Robinson will be present.

Episode C.

This meeting will be very briefly summarized—these men being only medium salaried and as a rule not very thoughtful men or very articulate men and are very easily bamboozled into taking this 50% cut that Bradogue is going to put over in Stahr's absence. At the end of the meeting, Robinson should be summoned from the meeting or called aside in almost a mysterious way suggesting to the reader that there is some significance in his being called away though this is a fact that will not be explained at this time. We will go from here to what I hope will be a big scene in which Bradogue asks the directors, writers, supervisors to accept a 50% cut which he says he is going to accept himself, using as his argument, to their surprise and rather to their confusion, the specious argument that by accepting this they will save those in the lower salary brackets—the secretaries from $12.

a week up and the prop boys, etc., to whom the drastic cut would mean a terrible hardship. He gets over his idea for two reasons—one because the amorphous unions—though the name is not used—which are called into being among workers with common interest such as directors and writers are split by jealousies and factual disagreements, certain of them for example, have never even thought of themselves as workers and some are haunted by the old fashioned dream of communism and Bradogue is wise enough to use every stop on the organ including personal ties to increase these differences and to rule by dividing. In any case, he wins his point to the great disgust of those of the writers who are the more politically advanced or the shrewdest and who detect in this a very definite manifestation of a class war reaching Hollywood.

Episode D.

We will go from here, by the very quickest way, to an office where Cecelia is talking to a secretary who happens to be a personal friend who has helped her as a reader and who was called to the office of the chief of secretaries and now we learn that the whole thing has been a frame-up—that a great proportion of the secretaries are going to be laid-off without warning, that extensive cuts are to be made in their pay of 40% instead of 50% but still the very things that he has made his point by promising to avoid, are going to happen. Women with families to support are going to find that they have scarcely enough with which to buy bread and that they are without jobs and no chance to get a job in any other studio for to a certain extent, other studios have waited for this studio to start cutting and then take the same steps.

———

When Stahr is sick he keeps saying give it back to the directors again. Don't leave it with these men. Give it back. I took it away from etc. (Rearrange)

———

"No brilliant idea was ever born in a conference room," he assured the Dane. "But a lot of silly ideas have died there," said Stahr.

———

"We've had that problem before with stage plays," said Stahr, "In 'Tattersall' we took all the hints of what had gone before and even shot two thousand feet of it. Finally we cut it all—that's why it was such a short picture. Sherwood knew when he wanted to start his play and he was right. When you extend a play with a prelude you're asking for it—you're including a lot of situations the playwright has already rejected. That's why he's reduced them to a mention. Why should we take that mention like one of those dried fish from Iceland and dip in water. You can make it swell but you can't bring it to life."

———

Stahr had a working of technics but because he had been head man for so long and so many apprentices had grown up during his sway more knowledge was attributed to him than he possessed. He accepted this as the easiest way and was an adept though cautious bluffer. In the dubbing room, which was for sound what the cutting room was for sight he worked by ear alone and was often lost amid the chorus of ever newer terms and slang (get this up). So on the stages. He watched the new processes of faking animated backgrounds. Moving pictures taken against the background of other moving pictures, with a secret child's approval. He could have understood easily enough often he preferred not to preserve a sensual acceptance when he saw the scene unfold in the rushes. There were smart young men about—Rienmund was one—who phrased their remarks to convey the impression that they understood everything about pictures. Not Stahr. When he interfered it was always from his own point of view not from theirs. Thus his function was different from Griffith in the early days who had been all things to every finished frame of film.

———

I'll pay for passion—so will the public. But it's rare, and it doesn't consist of being born on Grand Street, and sometimes it wears out.

———

Incident of Stahr calmly telling off an agent he was an overgrown errand boy. Implication, you can get away with it with writers who are soft but not with him. Something like quarrel of Knopf with Swanie.

———

There is a place for a hint somewhere of a big agent to complete the picture. Myron or Berg though—no mercy for Swanson.

———

In order to forgive Stahr for what he did that afternoon it should be remembered that he came out of the old Hollywood that was rough and tough and where the wildest bluffs hold. He had manufactured gloss and polish and contour of new Hollywood but occasionally he liked to tear it apart just to see if it was there.

———

Never wanted his name on pictures—"I don't want my name on the screen because credit is something that should be given to others. If you are in a position to give credit to yourself then you do not need it."

———

The situation on the big lot was that every producer, director, and scenarist there could adduce proof that he was a money maker. With the phenomenal rise of the industry, the initial distrust of it by business, the stage and literature changing with the weeding out of better men from the needs of speed, with the emphasis as in a mining camp on the lower virtues; then with the growing complication of technique and the exclusiveness it created and finally with the grand consolidation and trashification whose finest flower was block booking—it could be fairly said of all and by all of those who remained that they had made money—despite the fact that most directors had been reduced by the talkies to mere putters on, that not a third of the producers or one twentieth of the writers could have earned their living in the East. That like the Boers army in the 19th century operating against ill-armed savages, scarcely a general, a colonel or a major was not one of these men, no matter how low grade and incompetent a fellow who could not claim to have participated largely in success. This made difficulty in dealing with them.

———

These blows hit Stahr all at once. But at first he has them in control. It is not till they hit his great picture which should be planted back in 10., that he realizes what they mean. He should quarrel with the writers in such a way as to effect the great pictures.

———

Paradox about Stahr the artist standing for reaction and corruption and—, and the people who stood for all the good things were horrible.

———

Some time passes slower for Stahr because of a quick heart and pulse. These seem more crowded days (like after the split)

———

The day Stahr died everyone on the lot (including the Marx Brothers) were crying and trying to see who was watching them. "Trash", I could hear him say. "Trash."

———

A scene where a communist insults Stahr *intolerably,* belittles his whole life.

———

These are the picture people. Do not blame them too much. I am sure you would do much better in their place if you had all that money to spend and that strange story of what happened to—to produce. We all have one story. But what would you do after that and that and that day after day after dozens hundreds thousands and ten thousands of time.

———

Let the glamor show as from far away. Cling to reality, for any departure from a high pitch of reality at which the Jews live leads to farce in which the Christians live. Hollywood is a Jewish holiday, a gentiles tragedy. Stahr should be half Jewish like Hunt. Or is this a compromise. I think it is.

———

In a strange atmosphere of a mining town in Lotus land.

———

Fitzgerald was undecided about having the plane wreckage looted by the children in the last chapter. This action was described in the synopsis sent to Littauer (pp. xii–xiii), but it is not stipulated in the outline. Fitzgerald explicated the thematic function of the looting material in a working note:

It is important that I begin this chapter with a delicate transition because I am not going to describe the Fall of the Plane but simply give a last picture of Stahr as the plane takes off and describe very briefly in the airport the people who are on board. The plane, therefore, has left for New York and when the reader turns to Chapter X, I must be sure that he isn't confused by the sudden change in scene and situation. Here I can make the best transition by an opening paragraph in which I tell the reader that Cecelia's story ends here and that what is now told was a situation discovered by the writer himself and pieced together from what he learned in a small town in Oklahoma, from a municipal judge. That the incidents occurred one month after the plane fell and plunged Stahr and all its occupants into a white darkness. Tell how the snow hid the wreck and that inspite of searching parties that the plane was considered lost and that will resume the narrative—that a curtain first went up during an early thaw the following March. (I have to go over all the chapters and get the time element to shape up so that Stahr's second trip to New York, the one on which he is killed, takes place when the first snow has fallen on the Rockies.* I want

———

*The Rocky Mountains are not in Oklahoma. Fitzgerald's reference below to "that particular atmosphere of Oklahoma when the long winter breaks" suggests that he had another locale in mind. *Editor.*

this plane to be like that plane that was lost for fully two months before they found the plane and the survivors). Consider carefully whether if possible by some technical trick, it might not be advisable to conceal from the reader that the plane fell until the moment when the children find it. The problem is that the reader must not turn to Chapter X and be confused, but on the other hand, the dramatic effect, even if the reader felt lost for a few minutes, might be more effective if he did not find at the beginning of the chapter that the plane fell. In fact, almost certainly that is the way to handle it and I must find a method of handling it in that fashion. There must be an intervening paragraph to begin Chapter X which will reassure the reader that he is following the same story, but it can be evasive and confine itself to leading the reader astray thinking that the paragraph is merely to explain that Cecelia is not telling this next part of the story without telling the reader that the plane ran into a mountain top and disappeared from human knowledge for several months.

When I have given the reader some sense of the transition and prepared him for a change in scene and situation, break the narrative with a space or so and begin the following story. That a group of children are starting off on a hike. That there is an early spring thaw in this mountain state. Pick out of the group of children three who we will call Jim, Frances and Dan. That atmosphere is that particular atmosphere of Oklahoma when the long winter breaks. The atmosphere must be an all cold climate where the winter breaks very suddenly with almost a violence—the snow seems to part as if very unwillingly in great convulsive movements like the break-up of an ice flow. There's a bright sun. The three children get separated from the teacher or scoutmaster or whoever is in charge of the expedition and the girl, Frances, comes upon a part of the engine and fly-wheel of a broken airplane. She has no idea what it is. She is rather puzzled by it and at the moment is engaged rather in a flirtation with both Jim and Dan. However, she is an intelligent child of 13 or 14 and while she doesn't identify it as part of an airplane she knows it is an odd piece of machinery to be found in the mountains. First she thinks it is the remains of some particular mining machinery. She calls Dan and then Jim and they forget whatever small juvenile intrigue they were embarking on in their discovery of other debris from the fall of the plane. Their first general instinct is to call the other members of the party because Jim who is the smartest of the children (both the boys ages about 15) recognizes that it is a fallen plane—though he doesn't connect it with the plane that disappeared the previous November) when Frances comes upon a purse and an open traveling case which belonged to the Lola Lane* actress. It contains the things that to her present undreamt of luxuries. In it there's a jewel box. It has been unharmed—it has fallen through the branches of a tree. There are flasks of perfume that would never appear in the town where she lives, perhaps a negligee or anything I can think of that an actress might be carrying which was absolutely the last word in film elegance. She is utterly fascinated.

Simultaneously Jim has found Stahr's briefcase. A briefcase is what he has always wanted and Stahr's briefcase is an excellent piece of leather and some other traveling appurtenances of Stahr's. Things that are notably possessions of wealthy men. I have no special ideas at present, but think what a very wealthy, well-equipped man might be liable to have with him on such an expedition and then Dan makes the suggestion of "Why do we have to tell about this? We can all come up here later and there is probably a lot more of this stuff here and there's probably money and everything." These people are dead—they will never need it again, then we can say about the plane or let other people find it. Nobody will know we have been up here."

Dan bears, in some form of speech, a faint resemblance to Bradogue.† This must be subtly done and not look too much like a parable or moral lesson, still the impression must be conveyed, but be careful to convey it once and rub it in. If the reader misses it, let it go—don't repeat. Show Frances as malleable and amoral in the situation, but show a definite doubt on Jim's part, even from the first, as to whether this is fair dealing even towards the dead. Close this episode with the children rejoining the party.

Several weeks later the children have now made several trips to the mountain and have rifled the place of everything that is of any value. Dan is especially proud of his find which includes some rather disreputable possessions of Ronciman.‡ Frances is worried and definitely afraid and tending to side with Jim who is now in an absolutely wretched mood about the whole affair. He knows that searching parties have been on a neighboring mountain—that the plane has been traced and that with the full flowering of spring the secret will come out and that each trip up, he feels that the danger is more and more. However, let that be Frances' feeling because Jim has, by this time, read the contents of Stahr's briefcase and late at night, taking it from the woodshed where he has concealed it has

---

*Lola Lane (1909–81) had leading roles in the movies during the Thirties. *Editor.*

†The name *Bradogue* and references to Chapter X confirm that this was an early memo-note. *Editor.*

‡One of the passengers, a shady movie producer. *Editor.*

gotten an admiration for the man. Naturally, by the time of this episode all three children are aware of what plane it was and who was in it and whose possessions they have.

One day also they have found the bodies, though I do not want to go into this scene in any gruesome manner, of the six or seven victims still half concealed by the snow. In any case, something in one of Stahr's letters that Jim reads late at night decides him to go to Judge ———— and tell the whole story which he does against the threats of Dan who is bigger than he is and could lick him physically. We leave the children there with the idea that they are in good hands, that they are not going to be punished, that having made full restoration and the fact that, after all they could plead in court that they did not know anything more about the situation than "finder's keeper's." There will be no punishment of any kind for any of the three children. Give the impression that Jim is all right— that Frances is faintly corrupted and may possibly go off in a year or so in search of adventure and may turn into anything from a gold digger to a prostitute and that Dan has been completely corrupted and will spend the rest of his life looking for a chance to get something for nothing.

I cannot be too careful not to rub this in or give it the substance or feeling of a moral tale. I should very pointedly that that Jim is all right and end perhaps with Frances and let the readers hope that Frances is going to be all right and then take that hope away by showing the last glimpse of Frances with that lingering conviction that luxury is over the next valley, therefore giving a bitter and acrid finish to the incident to take away any possible sentimental and moral stuff that may have crept into it. Certainly end the incident with Frances.

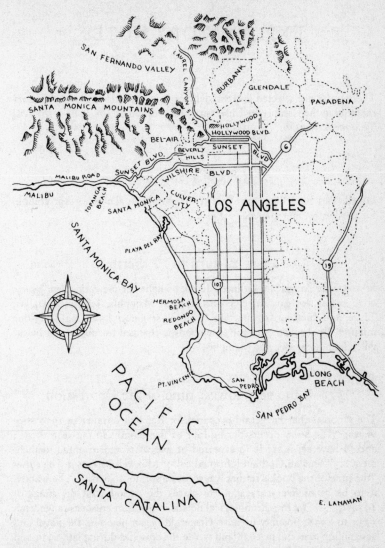

The geography of *The Love of the Last Tycoon* (map by Eleanor Lanahan).

EXPLANATORY NOTES

These notes are selected and revised from the comprehensive explanatory material in the Cambridge University Press edition of *The Love of the Last Tycoon: A Western*.

3.8 Lolly Parsons

Louella Parsons (1880–1972), writer of an influential movie gossip column for the Hearst newspapers. (see also 129.34).

4.12, 24 turn in . . . berth

In 1936 the American Airlines Mercury Flight left Newark, New Jersey, at 6:10 P.M. for Los Angeles with stops at Memphis, Tennessee; Dallas, Texas; and Tucson, Arizona. The trip took seventeen hours and forty-one minutes. By August 1937 the schedule was changed to substitute a Nashville, Tennessee, stop for Memphis.

5.7–8 the very lowest time of the Depression

The synopsis that Fitzgerald prepared for Kenneth Littauer in 1939 stipulates: "The Story occurs during four or five months in the year 1935"; and "I have set it safely in a period of five years ago to obtain detachment . . ." Sheilah Graham informed editor Maxwell Perkins in 1941 that "the time of the book's setting was most important to Scott . . . he wanted it to be as of five years ago. He places the period with the songs of 1934–5 . . ." Yet the chronological details in the draft episodes range from 1933 to 1938, possibly because Fitzgerald began planning the novel and assembling material in 1938 and wrote the episodes during late 1939 and 1940—so that the time of the novel changed during the course of composition.

The first time signal appears on p. 5 where "the very lowest time of the Depression" (which began after the October 1929 stock market crash) is placed "two years before" the present time of the novel—that is, any year from 1933 to 1935. On p. 8 Cecelia refers to the 1935 songs "Top Hat" and "Cheek to Cheek" as having been popular when she was a freshman;

since she is a junior at the time of the novel (although it is not clear whether she has completed her junior year or is a rising junior), the year would be 1937 or 1938. On p. 27 there is a reference to "the three years of Depression"—which places the action in 1932 or 1933. Other songs—"Lost" and "Gone"—were published in 1936. The reference to Wallis Warfield Simpson on p. 116 establishes the time as later; Edward VIII abdicated in 1936 and as the Duke of Windsor married Mrs. Simpson in June 1937. The latest datable detail in the novel is the reference to Superman on p. 124. This cartoon character was introduced in *Action Comics* in spring 1938, and the first *Superman* comic book appeared in 1939.

The year in which the events of the novel transpire cannot be established. Disregarding the references to Superman and to Mrs. Simpson, *The Love of the Last Tycoon* can be conveniently thought of as taking place during the summer of 1936. On p. 12 Cecelia states that she is reporting events that occurred "five years ago"; since Fitzgerald expected to publish his novel in 1941, the year 1936 fits the interior time scheme.

5.21–3 bonus army

In 1932 thousands of World War I veterans came to Washington, D.C., and demanded early payment of their veterans' bonuses; they were dispersed by troops.

11.20 lotus land

A place of luxury and voluptuous idleness; eating the lotus induced forgetfulness of home in the *Odyssey*.

12.17–19 Old Hickory . . . New Orleans . . . National Bank . . . Spoils System

Andrew Jackson (1767–1845), popularly known as Old Hickory, defeated the British at the Battle of New Orleans (1815); during his presidency (1828–36) the Bank of the United States was terminated, and his political supporters were rewarded with government jobs.

14.4 iron maidens

Coffin-shaped torture instruments that drove spikes through the victims.

16.4 the Bronx

The Bronx at the time of Stahr's boyhood, before World War I, was largely populated by lower-middle-class families—including many Jews who had left Manhattan's Lower East Side. A passage on p. 115 indicates that Stahr's early boyhood was spent in Erie, Pennsylvania.

20.29—30 all the kingdoms

Echo of Luke 4:15: "And the devil, taking him up into an high mountain, shewed unto him all the kingdoms of the world in a moment of time" (King James version).

21.18 John Swanson

Based on cowboy actor Harry Carey (1878–1947), a star of the silent movies who became a character actor in sound movies.

26.6 god Siva

The third person in the Hindu triad, with Brahma and Vishnu, Siva represents the principle of destruction and reconstruction; he is also the god of the arts. Fitzgerald's drafts refer to Siva as a goddess.

27.24 Emperor . . . Old Guard

The most honored regiment of Napoleon's Imperial Guard, formed between 1800 and 1806 and made up of veterans; Fitzgerald may be referring to Horace Vernet's painting, "Napoleon's Farewell at Fontainebleau."

28.11 drummer's sense of story

Drummers—traveling salesmen—were identified with vulgar anecdotes of seduction.

29.5 gone to pot

Undergone a process of deterioration; the use of *pot* as slang for marijuana was not yet current.

29.35–6 *Tout passe.—L'art robuste / Seul a l'éternité.*

From Théophile Gautier's poem "L'Art" (1858): "Everything perishes. Only strong art endures."

35.17 Claris

Presumably the name of a brothel or a madame.

41.2 Hays office

Will H. Hays (1879–1954), president 1922–45 of the Motion Picture Producers and Distributors of America, the industry's self-censorship office; he compiled its 1930 Production Code.

43.3 Joe Breen

Joseph Breen (1890–1965) was associated with Will Hays at the Motion Picture Producers and Distributors Association of America.

44.29 Prince Agge

Prince Aage of Denmark (d. 1940) was the cousin of King Christian and the nephew of Queen Alexandra of England; he renounced his rights to the throne of Denmark in 1914. Prince Aage wrote *A Royal Adventurer in the Foreign Legion* (1927) and *Fire by Day and Flame by Night* (1937). During 1934–38 Count Sigvard Bernadotte of Sweden was an assistant director at M-G-M. As Fitzgerald's reference to the House of Bernadotte (the royal house of Sweden) suggests, he probably conflated Prince Aage with Count Bernadotte of Sweden.

48.31 Nicolay's biography

John G. Nicolay and John Hay, *Abraham Lincoln: A History* (New York: Century, 1890), an admiring biography by men who knew Lincoln.

51.11 Miss Foodstuffs

A phrase used by Stahr to indicate the blandness of the actress's filmed performance.

53.17 *coureur du bois*

A French fur trader in Canada.

61.10–11 Diogenes . . . Asclepius . . . Menanader

Fitzgerald's latest draft reads "Diocenes . . . Esculpias . . . Minanorus." Diogenes (fourth century B.C.) was a Greek Cynic philosopher; Asclepius was the Greek god of medicine; Minanorus has not been identified, but Fitzgerald was probably referring to the Greek comic dramatist Menander (third century B.C.). Wilson altered Fitzgerald's readings to "Euripides . . . Aristophanes . . . Menander."

61.20–1 Eleusinian mysteries

Forms of worship celebrated in ancient Greece at Eleusis in Attica in honor of Demeter, Persephone, and Dionysius. Zavras's ironic hyperbole identifies the studio administration with gods.

66.13 reefer

British term for a close-fitting jacket of heavy cloth.

68.27 last man tapped for Bones

Skull and Bones is a senior society or "secret society" at Yale University that elects fifteen undergraduates each year at a ritual known as Tap Day. Election to Bones was regarded as the highest social distinction at Yale, and it was a particular honor to be the fifteenth man tapped.

74.10–11 Grand Street . . . Loudoun County

Street in the Lower East Side of Manhattan and at that time a poor Jewish neighborhood; county in rural northern Virginia, near the Maryland line. These locations indicate the variety of backgrounds of the movie people.

74.31 dancing with the Prince of Wales

When Edward VIII (1894–1972) was the bachelor Prince of Wales (1911–36), dancing with him was a coveted experience and inspired the 1928 song "I've Danced With a Man, Who Danced With a Girl, Who Danced With the Prince of Wales"—music by Herbert Farjeon, lyrics by Harold Scott.

81.24 cheaters

Slang for sunglasses.

91.13 Venus on the half shell

The painting "The Birth of Venus" by Italian artist Sandro Botticelli (1445–1510) depicts Venus on a large scallop shell, and it is jocularly referred to as "Venus on the half shell" in reference to menu terminology.

91.31 Spengler

Oswald Spengler (1880–1936), author of *The Decline of the West* (translated into English 1926–28), an erudite work of history and philosophy that influenced Fitzgerald.

92.4 shuls

Yiddish word that means schools and synagogues.

100.27–8 In disgrace with fortune and men's eyes

From Shakespeare's Sonnet 29.

103.4 skivies and biddies

Skivies (skivvies) are scullery maids; biddies are chambermaids.

107.4 Lord Charnwood

Godfrey Rathbone Benson, Lord Charnwood (1864–1945), author of *Abraham Lincoln* (London: Constable, 1916).

107.8 "A productions"

High-budget movies, as differentiated from cheaper B productions.

113.17 Black and Tans

Special constables recruited in England in 1920 to suppress the Irish rebellion; their uniforms were khaki trousers and black tunics, or vice versa. They became notorious for their reprisals against the Irish Republican Army.

114.14 syndicalist

Member of a radical movement that seeks to gain worker control over production.

117.35 Jews were dead miserably

Victims of the violent anti-Semitism that accompanied Hitler's appointment as Chancellor of Germany in 1933 and escalated thereafter, being legitimized by the anti-Jewish "Nuremberg Laws" adopted in September 1935. Fitzgerald is not referring to the "Final Solution"; he had been dead seven months when in July 1941 the extermination of the Jews became official Nazi policy.

118.15 Harry Bridges

Australian-born American labor leader (1901–90), head of the West-coast International Longshoremen's Association and later of the International

Longshoremen's and Warehousemen's Union; he denied Communist Party membership but supported its positions.

118.22 "I AM" cult

An occult faith founded in California in 1929; the term "I AM" designates the Primal Light or the energy of God, the basis for all manifested form.

119.1 Writers Guild

The first Screen Writers Guild was established in 1920; it was reorganized in 1933 as an organization that would give writers more control over story material. The leftist contingent in the Screen Writers Guild pushed for amalgamation with other writers' unions—the Authors' League, the Dramatists' Guild, the Newspaper Guild, and the Radio Writers Guild. Irving Thalberg opposed the Screen Writers Guild.

123.5 Company Tec

Private detective or policeman on the company payroll.

123.27 Frankensteen

Richard Frankensteen (1907–   ) and Walter Reuther, United Auto Workers union officials, were beaten by Ford strikebreakers in the May 1937 Detroit "Battle of the Overpass." Although described in the novel as "this big Jew," Frankensteen is an Episcopalian.

125.19 Legion of Decency

Roman Catholic board organized in 1934 to combat immorality in movies; the organization prepared lists of movies unfit for Catholics.

126.22 Fitts

Buron Fitts, District Attorney for Los Angeles County in the Thirties, was allegedly in the pay of the studios.

FURTHER READING

The Love of the Last Tycoon: A Western, ed. Bruccoli. Cambridge & New York: Cambridge University Press, 1993. Scholarly edition with full editorial apparatus.

F. Scott Fitzgerald Manuscripts, 18 vols., ed. Bruccoli. New York & London: Graland, 1990–1991; Vol. 5, Parts 1–3.

The Pat Hobby Stories. New York: Scribners, 1962.

The Romantic Egoists: A Pictorial Autobiography from the Scrapbooks and Albums of F. Scott and Zelda Fitzgerald, ed. Scottie Fitzgerald Smith, Joan P. Kerr & Bruccoli. New York: Scribners, 1974.

F. Scott Fitzgerald: A Life in Letters, ed. Bruccoli. New York: Scribners, 1994.

Bruccoli. *"The Last of the Novelists": F. Scott Fitzgerald and The Last Tycoon.* Carbondale & Edwardsville: Southern Illinois University Press, 1977.

Bruccoli. *Some Sort of Epic Grandeur: The Life of F. Scott Fitzgerald,* Revised edition. New York: Carroll & Graf, 1992.

Bruccoli. *F. Scott Fitzgerald: A Descriptive Bibliography, Revised Edition.* Pittsburgh: University of Pittsburgh Press, 1987.

A BRIEF LIFE OF
F. SCOTT FITZGERALD

The compensation of a very early success is a conviction that life is a romantic matter.

—F. Scott Fitzgerald

The dominant influences on F. Scott Fitzgerald were aspiration, literature, Princeton, Zelda Sayre Fitzgerald, and alcohol.

Francis Scott Key Fitzgerald was born in St. Paul, Minnesota, on September 24, 1896, the namesake and second cousin three times removed of the author of the National Anthem. Fitzgerald's given names indicate his parents' pride in his father's ancestry. His father, Edward, was from Maryland, with an allegiance to the old South and its values. Fitzgerald's mother, Mary (Mollie) McQuillan, was the daughter of an Irish immigrant who became wealthy as a wholesale grocer in St. Paul. Both were Catholics.

Edward Fitzgerald failed as a manufacturer of wicker furniture in St. Paul, and he became a salesman for Procter & Gamble in upstate New York. After he was dismissed in 1908, when his son was twelve, the family returned to St. Paul and lived comfortably on Mollie Fitzgerald's inheritance. Fitzgerald attended the St. Paul Academy; his first writing to appear in print was a detective story in the school newspaper when he was thirteen.

During 1911–13 he attended the Newman School, a Catholic prep school in New Jersey, where he met Father Sigourney Fay, who encouraged his ambitions for personal distinction and achievement. As a member of the Princeton Class of 1917, Fitzgerald neglected his studies for his literary apprenticeship. He wrote the scripts and lyrics for the Princeton Triangle Club musicals and was a contributor to the *Princeton Tiger* humor magazine and the *Nassau Literary Magazine*. His college friends included Edmund Wilson and John Peale Bishop. On academic probation and unlikely to graduate, Fitzgerald joined the army in 1917 and was commissioned a second lieutenant in the infantry. Convinced that he would die in the war, he rapidly wrote a novel, "The Romantic Egotist"; the letter of rejection from Charles Scribner's Sons praised the novel's originality and asked that it be resubmitted when revised.

In June 1918 Fitzgerald was assigned to Camp Sheridan, near Montgomery, Alabama. There he fell in love with a celebrated belle, eighteen-year-old Zelda Sayre, the youngest daughter of an Alabama Supreme Court judge. The romance intensified Fitzgerald's hopes for the success of his novel, but after revision it was rejected by Scribners a second time. The war ended just before he was to be sent overseas; after his discharge in 1919 he went to New York City to seek his fortune in order to marry. Unwilling to wait while Fitzgerald succeeded in the advertisement business and unwilling to live on his small salary, Zelda broke their engagement.

In July 1919 Fitzgerald quit his job and returned to St. Paul to rewrite his novel as *This Side of Paradise;* it was accepted by editor Maxwell Perkins of Scribners in September. Set mainly at Princeton and described by its author as "a quest novel," *This Side of Paradise* traces the career aspirations and love disappointments of Amory Blaine.

In the fall-winter of 1919 Fitzgerald commenced his career as a writer of stories for the mass-circulation magazines. Working through agent Harold Ober, Fitzgerald interrupted work on his novels to write money-making popular fiction for the rest of his life. *The Saturday Evening Post* became Fitzgerald's best story market, and he was regarded as a "*Post* writer." His early commercial stories about young love introduced a fresh character: the independent, determined young American woman who appeared in "The Offshore Pirate" and "Bernice Bobs Her Hair." Fitzgerald's more ambitious stories, such as "May Day" and "The Diamond as Big as the Ritz," were published in *The Smart Set,* which had a small circulation.

The publication of *This Side of Paradise* on March 26, 1920, made the twenty-four-year-old Fitzgerald famous almost overnight, and a week later he married Zelda in New York. They embarked on an extravagant life as young celebrities. Fitzgerald endeavored to earn a solid literary reputation, but his playboy image impeded the proper assessment of his work.

After a riotous summer in Westport, Connecticut, the Fitzgeralds took an apartment in New York City; there he wrote his second novel, *The Beautiful and Damned,* a naturalistic chronicle of the dissipation of Anthony and Gloria Patch. When Zelda became pregnant they took their first trip to Europe in 1921 and then settled in St. Paul for the birth of their only child; Frances Scott (Scottie) Fitzgerald was born in October 1921.

Fitzgerald expected to become affluent from his play, *The Vegetable;* in the fall of 1922 they moved to Great Neck, Long Island, in order to be near Broadway. The political satire—subtitled "From President to Postman"—failed at its tryout in November 1923, and Fitzgerald wrote his way out of debt with short stories. The distractions of Great Neck and New York prevented Fitzgerald from making progress on his third novel. During this time his drinking increased. Fitzgerald was an alcoholic, but he wrote sober. Zelda regularly got "tight," but she was not an alcoholic. There were frequent domestic rows, usually triggered by drinking bouts.

Literary opinion-makers were reluctant to accord Fitzgerald full marks as a serious craftsman. His reputation as a drinker inspired the myth that he was an irresponsible writer; yet he was a painstaking reviser whose fiction went through layers of drafts. Fitzgerald's clear, lyrical, colorful, witty style evoked the emotions associated with time and place. When critics objected to Fitzgerald's concern with love and success, his response was: "But, my God! it was my material, and it was all I had to deal with." The chief theme of Fitzgerald's work is aspiration—the idealism he regarded as defining American character. Another major theme was mutability or loss. As a social historian Fitzgerald became identified with "The Jazz Age": "It was an age of miracles, it was an age of art, it was an age of excess, and it was an age of satire."

The Fitzgeralds went to France in the spring of 1924 seeking tranquillity for his work. He wrote *The Great Gatsby* during the summer and fall in Valescure near St. Raphael, but the marriage was damaged by Zelda's involvement with a French naval aviator. The extent of the affair—if it was in fact consummated—is not known. On the Riviera the Fitzgeralds formed a close friendship with Gerald and Sara Murphy.

The Fitzgeralds spent the winter of 1924–25 in Rome, where he revised *The Great Gatsby;* they were en route to Paris when the novel was published in April. *The Great Gatsby* marked a striking advance in Fitzgerald's technique, utilizing a complex structure and a controlled narrative point of view. Fitzgerald's achievement received critical praise, but sales of *Gatsby* were disappointing, though the stage and movie rights brought additional income.

In Paris Fitzgerald met Ernest Hemingway—then unknown outside the expatriate literary circle—with whom he formed a friendship based largely on his admiration for Hemingway's personality and genius. The Fitzgeralds remained in France until the end of 1926, alternating between Paris and the Riviera.

Fitzgerald made little progress on his fourth novel, a study of American expatriates in France provisionally titled "The Boy Who Killed His Mother," "Our Type," and "The World's Fair." During these years Zelda's unconventional behavior became increasingly eccentric.

The Fitzgeralds returned to America to escape the distractions of France. After a short, unsuccessful stint of screen writing in Hollywood, Fitzgerald rented "Ellerslie," a mansion near Wilmington, Delaware, in the spring of 1927. The family remained at "Ellerslie" for two years interrupted by a visit to Paris in the summer of 1928, but Fitzgerald was still unable to make significant progress on his novel. At this time Zelda commenced ballet training, intending to become a professional dancer. The Fitzgeralds returned to France in the spring of 1929, where Zelda's intense ballet work damaged her health and estranged them. In April 1930 she suffered her first breakdown. Zelda was treated at Prangins clinic in Switzerland until September 1931, while Fitzgerald lived in Swiss hotels. Work on the novel was again suspended as he wrote short stories to pay for psychiatric treatment.

Fitzgerald's peak story fee of $4,000 from *The Saturday Evening Post* may have had in 1929 the purchasing power of $40,000 in 1994 dollars.

Nonetheless, the general view of his affluence is distorted. Fitzgerald was not among the highest-paid writers of his time; his novels earned comparatively little, and most of his income came from 160 magazine stories. During the 1920s his income from all sources averaged under $25,000 a year—good money at a time when a schoolteacher's average annual salary was $1,299, but not a fortune. Scott and Zelda Fitzgerald did spend money faster than he earned it; the author who wrote so eloquently about the effects of money on character was unable to manage his own finances.

The Fitzgeralds returned to America in the fall of 1931 and rented a house in Montgomery. Fitzgerald made a second unsuccessful trip to Hollywood in 1931. Zelda suffered a relapse in February 1932 and entered Johns Hopkins Hospital in Baltimore. She spent the rest of her life as a resident or outpatient of sanitariums.

In 1932, while a patient at Johns Hopkins, Zelda rapidly wrote *Save Me the Waltz*. Her autobiographical novel generated considerable bitterness between the Fitzgeralds, for he regarded it as pre-empting the material that he was using in his novel-in-progress. Fitzgerald rented "La Paix," a house outside Baltimore, where he completed his fourth novel, *Tender Is the Night*. Published in 1934, his most ambitious novel was a commercial failure, and its merits were matters of critical dispute. Set in France during the 1920s, *Tender Is the Night* examines the deterioration of Dick Diver, a brilliant American psychiatrist, during the course of his marriage to a wealthy mental patient.

The 1935–37 period is known as "the crack-up" from the title of an essay Fitzgerald wrote in 1936. Ill, drunk, in debt, and unable to write commercial stories, he lived in hotels in the region near Asheville, North Carolina, where in 1936 Zelda entered Highland Hospital. After Baltimore Fitzgerald did not maintain a home for Scottie. When she was fourteen she went to boarding school, and the Obers became her surrogate family. Nonetheless, Fitzgerald functioned as a concerned father by mail, attempting to supervise Scottie's education and to shape her social values.

Fitzgerald went to Hollywood alone in the summer of 1937 with a six-month Metro-Goldwyn-Mayer contract at $1,000 a week. He received his only screen credit for adapting *Three Comrades* (1938), and his contract was renewed for a year at $1,250 a week. This $91,000 from M-G-M was a great deal of money during the late Depression years when a new Chevrolet coupé cost $619, but, although Fitzgerald paid off his debts, he was unable to save. His trips East to visit Zelda were disastrous. In California Fitzgerald fell in love with movie columnist Sheilah Graham. Their relationship endured despite his benders. After M-G-M dropped his option at the end of 1938, Fitzgerald worked as a freelance script writer and wrote short-short stories for *Esquire*. He began his Hollywood novel, *The Love of the Last Tycoon*, in 1939 and had written more than half of a working draft when he died of a heart attack in Graham's apartment on December

21, 1940. Zelda Fitzgerald perished in a fire in Highland Hospital in 1948.

F. Scott Fitzgerald died believing himself a failure. The obituaries were condescending, and he seemed destined for literary obscurity. The first phase of the Fitzgerald resurrection—"revival" does not properly describe the process—occurred between 1945 and 1950. By 1960 he had achieved a secure place among America's enduring writers: *The Great Gatsby,* a work that seriously examines the theme of aspiration in an American setting, defines the classic American novel.

M.J.B.